THE ROOT OF ALL EVIL

When Bartholomew Denton, the owner of Leaham Hall in North Yorkshire, is discovered dead in his bed, Detection Officer Sergeant Hector Blagdon is called in. Young and fit as Denton was, the death seems suspicious. Blagdon is also intrigued by the quick turnover of maid-servants at the Hall, and wonders if there is something else going on. With his old adversary Kendel the butler seemingly trying to frustrate the investigation, Blagdon must delve deep to find answers . . .

VALERIE HOLMES

THE ROOT OF ALL EVIL

Complete and Unabridged

LINFORD
Leicester

First published in Great Britain in 2018

First Linford Edition
published 2018

A catalogue record for this book is available
from the British Library.

ISBN 978–1–4448–3731–5

Published by
F. A. Thorpe (Publishing)
Anstey, Leicestershire

Set by Words & Graphics Ltd.
Anstey, Leicestershire
Printed and bound in Great Britain by
T. J. International Ltd., Padstow, Cornwall

This book is printed on acid-free paper

1

Leaham Hall, North Yorkshire
Tuesday, 30th April 1912

'I understand it was a young maid who found the body?' I stated, as I stepped onto the centuries-worn stone flagged floor of Leaham Hall's kitchens. Having been commanded by Frederick Kendel, the butler, to leave my bicycle outside the dairy and walk across the cobbled yard by the stables to the kitchens, I was in no mood to be given further instruction. He walked ahead of me, but did not speak. I glared at his back, hoping he could feel the years of resentment I held for him burning between those proud shoulderblades. My ride here had been long, cold and tiring.

Ducking under a low arch — well, too low for my six-foot frame to stride through at full height, although I noticed Kendel managed it without correcting his upright posture — I avoided catching my head on its hard edge. I found the Hall's staff standing by the kitchen's oven. At least they were being kept warmed against the chill of the day. I shouldn't complain really, none of us should, as it had not been a cold year so far. I subdued my anger and self-pity as I recalled the horrific headlines which had made me realise how awful it would have been for the poor sods that only weeks earlier had died a terrifying freezing death on the 'unsinkable' ship Titanic as it sank into the icy ocean.

'This way,' he said, staring at my muddied shoes.

I didn't care for Kendel's manner, but then I never had. He had always been a brute of a man, so how he had gained a trusted position in a house such as this confounded me.

I already knew it was the pretty young maid, Ivy, who had found Mr Denton's prone corpse. The message received from the household had stated this. The girl should be traumatised by her experience. He was too young to die, only in his mid-thirties if he was a day, and owner of the impressive Jacobean Hall and its surrounding wealthy estate. It had existed for decades, and included prosperous local mills and mines. I gritted my teeth. The family had lived in the area for generations, like mine, but there the similarity ended. My father had worked and died in one of Denton's mines. At least now the reality of strikes had resulted in a minimum wage for the souls who still toiled in them, rarely seeing the light of day. Surprisingly, I had to choke back the memory of the day Mother had been told that the explosion had killed Father along with my older brother Jeb. He definitely had been too young to die. My face was still red from the cold and exertion of my journey here, so the unexpected wave of emotion that swept through my veins was hidden from the eyes that now focused upon me.

It was the scared, cobalt blue eyes staring back at mine from a pale face, framed by pretty blonde curls that were neatly trapped within a cotton cap, that touched my heart. Young Ivy scrunched up the edge of her matching starched white apron as she answered my question.

'Aye, I found him . . . just lying there, staring . . . ' Ivy almost snapped her words out. That made me realise that there was some other emotion wrapped around her answer — surely it couldn't be anger? The voice was not as wavering as her hands were shaky. Deep within this young woman, I suspected, was a strength of will that somehow defied her fifteen years. She was undoubtedly nervous, but I knew appearances could also be very deceptive, especially where female guile was concerned — though this one was perhaps too young to have mastered it.

'Tell me how and when you found him.' I scanned the other anxious faces — the cook, laundry and upstairs maids, a young stable lad, and Kendel. I was wondering where the housekeeper was. The staff was quite small, but then I supposed that the Hall had run around the Denton family like clockwork for years. Fewer people wanted to accept a life of complete servitude. Like many other people, I felt times were changing in the world for these estates.

The girl, Ivy, kept glaring back at me. Why was she so direct — bold, even? Her attitude belied her age and sex. I wondered what other story lurked inside that pretty head. Could I get her to share it?

'Manners, girl,' said Mrs Elmwood the cook, said shaking her head. 'Forgive her, she's all upset, Sergeant Blagdon. We all are. You see, it was like this: he woke up dead, he did, and Ivy was first to see him when she went to light the fire in his room and take him his morning coffee.' She shrugged as if it was all beyond her comprehension.

I raised a brow at this, but she misunderstood the reason why.

'It was a disgusting habit that he picked up in Boston, I'm told. He was always insistent on a nice hot drink of strong sweet coffee for when he woke.' She sniffed, but covered her face as she did so. 'Ivy took it in to him.'

As Cook stepped up to the side of the young woman, I stifled the urge to smile. He did not wake up at all — that was the mystery to be solved. Dead men don't wake, they don't sleep — they just are. The two women stood just inside the arch of the stone kitchen, both watching me very carefully. Curious, I thought. Suspicious, I definitely was.

Kendel interrupted me. 'She has already told me all the details you need to know. Why are you here, Hector? I cannot imagine why you would pedal all that distance on that contraption at a time of such grief for Mrs Denton. We should have just sent for the family doctor. I was only in the library; it is my position that has been usurped here. They should have come straight to me and asked permission to use the telephone. Dr Marks has been Mr Denton's doctor for thirty-seven years. He was there at the man's birth. It was only correct that he should be here at the poor man's sudden and early death. You should not be interfering at such a time as this. Please leave right now!' He actually stepped back and extended his arm toward the archway that led back out to the door and the cobbled yard beyond. I was damned if I was going to be ordered about by this pompous ass.

'I am a Detection Officer, Kendel,' I corrected him and saw the man's back instantly stiffen. 'I am here because a death has been reported, and we do not know the cause of it just yet. As I am here officially, I will be staying until my job is done. That is precisely why our police doctor will see the body first. We insist upon this as routine, and it is why a call to another doctor, no matter how well connected they are to the family, is ill-advised. Once Dr Jackman has studied the corpse *in situ*, a decision will be made as to where it should be taken next, and when — or if — it can be released to the family for arrangements to go ahead.' I stared at him, daring him to challenge me; wondering if he had personal reasons to want to keep me away from his master's body.

'Well . . . Detection Officer Blagdon, I most certainly would not have called for you!' He glanced at the cook, who gave a slight shrug of her shoulders. 'The doctor will determine the cause, and not some local flatfoot Jack! We will go to Mr Denton's study . . . ' He cleared his throat and added, 'The study,' as if the man whose body lay undisturbed in his bedchamber no longer had ownership, or indeed any right to have his name mentioned in his own home. 'There, I will give you all the details you need to report back to your superiors, and the girl can be about her tasks. Idle hands are free for the devil's work to begin. They are no good at a time like this.'

I wondered what devil's work, if any, accounted for the master's sudden death.

Kendel continued, undeterred by my authority or my words, 'I'll make arrangements for the body to be removed, and also to inform his uncle in Mayfair of this unfortunate and tragic loss. He has no other relatives that I am aware of, other than his wife.' He turned to leave, but hesitated when I did not move. 'Detection Officer Blagdon, this way!' he snapped, but I still did not shift. The man was full of arrogance, so I decided it was time it was dented.

I continued to watch Ivy. Mrs Elmwood, the cook, had a protective arm on the small of the young woman's back; but for all her apparent shock and fear, Ivy stood upright. I noticed that she stood centred on her own feet instead of leaning into the security of the older woman. Despite his insulting words, I stayed calm; he did not intimidate me. Kendel was nothing to me, he never was, and I had been called much worse in my years in the force than a flatfooted detective. It was almost true, except I had a bicycle, and aspirations to rise further in the force I was so proud of.

'Yes, Kendel, I intended to use the study. But your presence will not be required. I would speak to Ivy first, and then each member of the staff in turn. I will then ring a bell when I need you to fetch the next servant in. Please provide me with a list of who was here last night and this morning. Do not touch the body or have it removed. I will be with the doctor when he arrives, and nothing will be done until this has happened. Do I make myself clear, Mr Kendel? This is a police investigation, not a household inconvenience!' I had not meant my voice to rise, but how else to make the fool realise that this was not about a childhood battle for authority? It was about a man's death, and murder could not yet be ruled out or ruled in — I had to keep an open mind until the case, if there was one, was closed.

'Mr Denton plainly died in his sleep. He must have drunk a dram too much and could not breathe. This is a shameful and dramatic enough circumstance to have revealed to the world, if it should leak out, without you playing detective and making it into something it is not! Think of his wife, the family name, and the estate . . . ' He raised his hands to stress his point, and I was somewhat surprised to realise he genuinely cared so much about the family's good name. I wondered why. After all, the man was just a servant like all the others. Was it his own position he feared for?

I had an official rank and a possible murder to solve, and he was a 'man's man' now without a man to serve. I subdued the anger I felt. 'You have my instructions. Until the doctor arrives, you will do as I request.'

Kendel's colour deepened — despite me knowing I was being churlish, it pleased me to think I had pierced his thick skin. He had been an unbearable snob at school, a bully who picked upon the smaller boys. That is, until I squared up to him and saved a lad from a thrashing at his hands. Kendel had never forgotten the black eye I gave him. He was two years my senior, but I was always tall for my age. We were opposites, always had been and always would be. I still have dark locks, where his fair hair had thinned and showed signs of greying. I was tall, and he stocky. I wanted to enforce the law and see justice done, whilst he merely wanted to dominate and dismiss any wrongdoing to preserve the status quo. I won, and he had lost. Nowadays, he lorded it over the young girls and women here as if he was the owner of the Hall — well, he was not the master, and I would remind him so.

Looking back at Ivy, I could not help but wonder if it was the sight of the body, or the touch of death on a young person's life, or the loss and uncertainty of her future that seemed to grieve her the most.

Or did she fear being discovered? I would listen closely to her words and take notes, as it was my job to do so. I aimed to find out who lied, and who had the motive to kill, who was guilty. The man had been healthy, keen on the sports of the gentry, so he was too young to have just died — although that was not unknown in very rare circumstances. Sudden death, unexplainable, did occasionally occur. I felt a rush of excitement like that of my younger days when, against my mother's strict orders, I freewheeled down Sutton Bank, laughing and holding on for dear life. Still, I was an officer of the law now, and not a foolish young lad. Beyond the odd theft, or fights breaking out in the new industrialised areas of the Tees, this was a rare case that needed some real detective work to ascertain the facts, and I was going to do my level best to discover the truth.

Cook pulled the girl closer to her. I thought the gesture to be one that was made as if she was trying to take control of the situation, rather than comforting the girl's distress. Ivy did not relax, but remained as stiff as a post. I found that strange. Ivy did not seem as though she was distraught; there was no sign of her sobbing. Instead, she had a silent air about her, as if it was the anger I sensed which had overwhelmed her rather than the shock or grief of finding Mr Denton.

'I will see the body first, Mr Kendel, and then you can send Ivy to me. Have you or anyone disturbed anything? Have any other members of staff been in the room?' I asked both Kendel and Mrs Elmwood, looking from one to another, forcing my mind to stay on the investigation as the tempting waft of broth in the pot she stirred crossed my nostrils . . . toying with my growling, empty stomach. I had been up since five a.m. The cut of cold ham on a slice of home-baked bread that I had eaten for breakfast with a mug of tea seemed like a distant memory. It was now ten-thirty in the morning, and it had taken me a long time to cycle the distance to the Hall against a strong wind. Even so, I had beaten police surgeon Dr Ivan Jackman who had been called to a case twenty miles away in Gorebeck, though at least the good doctor had a motor vehicle. I envied him the luxury of driving a Vulcan. I aimed to have a motorcycle soon. Perhaps, if I solved the mystery of this man's death — if there was one to be disclosed — it would make a good case for me to be given one. I was an optimistic person.

'No . . . Do you want me to tidy him up a bit for the doctor?' Mrs Elmwood asked. 'I had to see to the lass first. Mrs Bellington is in such a state, but she won't take anything for her nerves.' She shook her head. 'She is so stubborn.'

Mr Kendel corrected her, which surprised me. 'She is not stubborn, Cook; she is a determined woman, and will deal with her emotions in the best way she can.'

'No, please don't touch the deceased. However, I would like to see the housekeeper Mrs Bellington as well, Kendel, after I have observed the body and spoken to Ivy — you could send her in next. By then, her determination may have won out over her emotional state.' I kept an impassive face, but my voice was deliberately firm. I was not being sarcastic.

Kendel squared up to me. A bold act for him, I knew. 'You will see the staff in the order I fetch them in to you. You do not summon our housekeeper after a lowly housemaid!' he blustered. 'We do things in the proper manner in this household. Everyone knows and abides by their rightful place in the natural scheme of things.'

'Mr Kendel, you do not understand; man, you will do as I say. The law requires that I investigate this situation as I see it is necessary to do so, and unless you mean to obstruct me in that process, I strongly suggest that you obey my orders.' I saw the young lad step behind Ivy as I asserted my authority. He obviously looked to her as an older sister figure. I could see a bond there in that one quick glance between them.

Kendel sighed heavily, and we moved into the corridor that led to the main hall. I followed, and stopped abruptly when he faced me. 'The man is dead. No one has declared it to be any more than an Act of God, yet you come in here playing detective . . . Dr Jackman will hear of this high-handedness, as will your superiors.'

'So do you intend to obstruct the law?' I asked. 'I come here to do my job, and I strongly suggest that you remember what yours is. Now waste no more time, man. Find the housekeeper and tell her to make herself ready to be interviewed . . . after I have seen the body and then spoken to Ivy.'

Kendel stormed off. I decided to linger a moment longer, and stepped back into the kitchens.

Cook nodded at me. 'Mrs Bellington ran directly in after Ivy screamed, and — well, to be honest, she went to pieces. God forgive me, I had no idea she had it in her till then!' Cook shook her head, but Ivy looked away, staring vacantly out of the window. 'She is a woman who knows her own mind, you see, not one that is given to fanciful notions or actions. Still, you don't see a dead man every day of the week, thank God, do you?'

'I will need to see Mrs Denton too.' My

request seemed simple enough.

I saw both women look at each other. The younger almost sneered, but the cook answered me. 'She has taken her medication,' Cook said, by way of explanation.

'Her medication?' I queried.

They nodded, but said nothing.

'Has she already been informed of his death? She was not in the bed alongside him?' I knew that people in society often slept in separate rooms; and, as she had not been mentioned by Ivy as being disturbed when she found the body, I presumed this to be the case. To me, it was a strange custom. There was nothing I loved more than snuggling up to my Elsie in a warm bed after a hard day dealing with God knew what, and cycling out in all weathers.

'She won't be awake for some while, I think, and then she may well be confused . . . She is most days when she takes her medication, I'm afraid.' Her eyes did not show the same understanding or compassion that her voice seemingly expressed. 'They have adjoining rooms, sir,' she explained.

'Why does she take the medication?' I asked, not liking what I was hearing. I knew Mrs Amelia Grace Denton. She was a delightful lady a few years older than her dead husband. He was in his late thirties, and she in her mid-forties. I was thirty-six, and definitely considered I had a lot of life left to live. Hopefully, a family of my own to have too! At the fair last summer, arranged by my lovely wife, Mrs Denton had been her usual graceful and elegant self. I had to admit I had quite a soft spot for her. Elsie was a domestically gifted woman who knew how to make a man a comfortable home, but Mrs Amelia Grace Denton was so different: the kind of woman I had never had the opportunity to talk to in the way I had with my wife. She had married below her rank, becoming a lady *in* the grand Hall instead of Lady *of* the grand Hall. She was the daughter of an earl, and her good breeding showed in every gesture she made. Grace by name and grace by nature, she knew how to make a man feel ten feet tall with one chance comment made to him — or, no doubt, reduce him to a lesser man inches lower than her with a single offhand dismissal. I had hidden my feelings well that day. In truth, although I was ashamed to admit it even to myself, I wanted to see her again. Her elegance was something I had never been so close to before, and I was quite smitten; but I had my Elsie now, and she was a real woman — not a fanciful dream, a kind and loving wife. What more could a man want?

I looked about me. 'Please show me where the body is, and I will speak to Mrs Denton as soon as she awakes.' I tried to sound determined, but I was distracted. Working on a near-empty stomach, my words, even to my own ears, lacked conviction. The smell of warmed broth along with the coffee brewing on the stove made my mouth salivate. I stopped and looked at both pots hopefully. The idea of sampling either would have kept me there a few moments longer, but instead Cook walked to the door.

'Ivy, clear the pots away, best keep busy. We shall have a simple meal today, prepared for those who can still stomach eating at such a time as this!' She cast an icy glare at me that I ignored. I doubted she went hungry often.

I stepped forward to follow her, but Ivy had paused for a moment. A marled tomcat snuck in as the rest of the staff left to be about their chores — all, that is, except the young lad.

'Atticus is hungry, Ivy,' he said hopefully. The fur ball wrapped itself around Ivy's skirts. Ivy saw it, ladled a scoop of the broth out, and placed the offering on an old tin plate before passing it to the lad. He smiled and placed it on the floor, discreetly dipping his own finger in the broth and sneaking a taste as he set the dish on the mat by the fire for the cat to lick up. Ivy showed no emotion, yet this caring gesture seemed automatic to her; so she had a kind heart, I thought. These two were definitely fond of each other, and that made me smile.

'If it caught more mice, it wouldn't be hungry, would it?' she said quickly, watching the door. I suspected it was an anxious look out for the return of Mrs Elmwood. Realising I had not left, she picked up the pot and placed it quickly in the washbowl.

The cat licked the plate clean. Happily, the lad fussed the animal, and then ran off with Atticus in playful pursuit.

Ivy, however, was less animated. As she stared out of the window, she stood as if transfixed, her fists clenched at her sides. She did not motion at all. Shock can be a devil to deal with, I thought. As a man grown, I had faced some horrific sights. She had gone into her master's room and found his corpse. Yet, despite knowing this would be an awful shock for her, something here seemed odd to me. Why would a young lass be going into a married man's bedroom, servant or not? Surely Kendel should have been the one to rouse his master, not a maid. The possibilities that filled my head were honest doubts about the human nature of a man in his prime, but they were far from honourable, and I had to dismiss them quickly in order to remain objective.

'Ivy, was there something you wished to say to me — to tell me?' I asked her, as Cook continued walking briskly away from me along the servants' passage.

The girl's pretty yet disturbed face turned towards me. She had a strange aura about her. Her eyes were rimmed with a line of red, brimming with unshed tears. I longed for her to reveal the secrets I was sure she held close to her heart.

'He promised me . . . all those words, and now . . . ' Her words tailed off, and she carried the rest of the pots over to the square stone sink by the window as Cook bobbed her head back around the door and snapped, 'Detection Officer, are you coming? Mr Kendel said he has been waiting for you in the study long enough . . . sir. He's a busy man, he says.' She grinned, apparently enjoying Kendel's discomfort. Seeing the obvious dislike that I had for him, and he for me, she seemed to be gloating as she watched a sparring match ensue before her.

I smiled at her, despite my thoughts being torn between images of my Elsie, with her down-to-earth, no-nonsense character; Mrs Amelia Grace Denton, with her fine ways and features; and the scared, desperately sad, cobalt eyes of a young wench in some obvious distress. I glanced back one last time, and saw Ivy's straightened back and the way her white knuckles clung onto the sink's edge. I determined that I would return to this fascinating, beguiling young woman soon. She had quite taken my mind off my empty stomach . . . or nearly. The cat, at least, was triumphant; it had purred and left happy. Lucky cat.

2

The deceased's bedroom was opposite the upper stairs. An impatient Kendel stood, arms crossed, waiting for me by the door.

'I know why you're doing this,' he snapped. 'You want to lord it up here to prove you have more authority over me. Well, out there — ' He pointed down the stairs to the main entrance. ' — you may do, but in here I rule this establishment . . . in Mr Denton's absence.' He cleared his throat as his voice cracked on the last four words.

'A man is dead, and it is my duty to do this,' I explained. 'That is the only reason, Kendel. Believe me, out there — ' I nodded towards the main door. ' — is a whole world that needs law keeping. I'd be happy to be out there in it and leave you in your small corner here, ruling your roost.'

'Be honest, man. I would have at least

credited you with that capability, to yourself if to no other. You want to besmirch the name of the Dentons because your father was blown to pieces in his father's mine. Well, I'll not stand by and let you do it. No doubt your brother lit the bloody gas lamp when he shouldn't have, and blew up with them!' His eyes bore into mine.

It was my turn to clench a fist. I could have landed him a punch that would have sent his heartless soul down those stairs so far that he landed at the gates of hell and not the main doors, but I was a man of the law and no vigilante. So I breathed deeply. I knew better than to react to his taunts. I had dealt with my grief long since.

He opened the door and walked in before me. I instinctively grimaced. Death has a smell of its own. It is almost palpable, and leaves one feeling heavy of heart.

The drapes were drawn; the four-poster bed was left as it had been discovered, with Denton lying across it. My eyes slowly adjusted to the gloom as Kendel pulled back one of the heavy drapes to let some daylight in. A bucket was discarded by the fire with cloth and coal. At the side of the bed, a tray had an upturned cup atop the marble and mahogany wash-stand.

The contents had apparently been spilt on the white linen pillowcase, carpet, and edge of the bedding. Denton's body lay prone, face-down, on the bed. I stared at the scene. There was a strong smell of vomit.

Kendel, as if reading my thoughts, explained. 'Mr Denton was ill last evening.' He cleared his throat. 'A tad too much to drink, I fear. He was relaxing in his own home, so that is hardly a crime — or surprising for a gentleman who has . . . *had* excellent taste in wine. He was left to rest as he seemed in need of sleep, only of course he did not . . . I had it cleaned up and his bedding changed; he was still fast asleep then, but the smell lingers.' His manner was gentler and more respectful to me here at the side of a dead man's bed than it had been since I arrived.

I looked at him, the bully of my childhood, who now seemed ill at ease and threatened by emotion as he looked at the body of Ms master.

I walked around the bed. 'Has he been moved at all?' I asked.

'No, the girl ran out. I met her and took her to Mrs Elmwood to get some sense out of her, then I came up here once I realised the gravity of her hysteria. It was obvious that he was dead. I felt his wrist for a pulse, and, well . . . he was as still and cold as ice. I had looked in on him around two a.m.; he was sleeping soundly then. Still warm and cosy . . . ' He cleared his throat and wiped his left eye with the back of his handkerchief, then quickly replaced it. I was quite taken aback to realise that he did have a heart after all.

The bell resounded from the front door, breaking into his comments. Instantly, the man who seemed to mourn his master was back to being the obnoxious butler. He stood straight, looked to the door, and strode out declaring, 'That will be your doctor, and so we shall have the poor man suitably cleaned and dressed ready for the funeral directors to see, as soon as he is done.' His manner had changed back to one of starch again.

'Do not make any assumptions just yet, Kendel. Wait till you are told what to do.' I looked at him and saw his colour rise. He really was taking my appearance badly. I wondered if it was the angst from our younger selves re-emerging, or if he had something to hide and wanted to drive me away because of it.

His head snapped back around. 'By whom? You? Mister Detection Officer? You are loving this, aren't you?' His words were spat out, dripping resentment.

I sighed. His bitterness was hardly apt for such a situation, yet if this was a case of murder and not death by natural causes, then perhaps it was the perfect place to see his true colours. 'No, I merely do my job.'

I stared at him. His emotions were high: anger; grief; jealousy? Who knew what drove a man like him? I aimed to find out.

He left. I was keen to have a look at the

body quickly before it was given over to the doctor to examine. I parted the hair below the temple. It was matted, but with stale vomit rather than the coffee which had supposedly been spilled with the girl's shock of seeing him. In fact, the stain on the pillow was under his face. Therefore, I realised he must have moved after she entered, or someone had pushed him over onto his side. He had rolled onto his front. For his hair to be matted in such a manner his body would have had to have been lying on his back. Already, something was seemingly amiss.

I could hear voices becoming louder as they approached the door. I stood back, listened, and waited.

'That blasted cat just ran out into the drive. What in hell's name was I supposed to do? Take flight? I hope you have my motor car cleaned whilst I am busy, and take care to polish it well. Stop that lad bawling his eyes out, I hardly did it on purpose. If the animal hadn't stopped in the middle of the drive to cough up furballs, I would not have run it over.' The doctor sounded more vexed than his normal calm manner. I knew the man well enough, as I drank with him once a week in The Flagon Inn. I realised he felt guilty and sorry for the boy. He was rarely flustered, yet the death of a cat and empathy for the lad had obviously affected him deeply, even though he dealt daily with human mortality.

So, Atticus was no more; the lad would indeed be distraught. Not such a lucky cat after all!

'Yes, sir, I certainly will. He is still upset about the news of Mr Denton's demise, I assure you. However, the cat is of no significance, and I will see to your car. In here, if you will, doctor. The local Constable is already protecting the deceased from further harm.'

The latter comment was said loudly as the door opened and with no little tinge of sarcasm.

'Ah, Hector, glad to see you!' My friend entered, and I felt hugely relieved, for I needed him to work with me on this case to give me time to interview the people who were in the house, before they had the chance to confer and cover themselves regarding any perceived wrongdoing. Time was of the essence, and this man knew how to use it to good effect. He was thorough, always keeping abreast of changes within his amazing field of detection. I studied the living, he the dead. Together we could reveal much.

I saw Kendel look on in disbelief. The greeting of my friend and colleague almost caused him to curl his lip. He obviously did not recognise one of his childhood victims, but I knew that Jackman had never forgotten him.

To make things worse, Dr Jackman turned to him, said, 'Thank you,' and casually dismissed him.

'If you bring Ivy to the study in ten minutes, I will come down and interview her,' I added as Kendel left without a word, closing the door behind him.

'Hasn't changed much, has he?' Ivan nodded towards the door.

'Ivan, you rile him cruelly.'

'Oh Hector, I feel bad about the cat. I was just trying to get here as quick as I could. Already seen one cadaver today.'

'Well, let's get started. Now, about our

victim . . . ' I returned to the matter in hand, only too aware that now the clock was truly ticking. Once Ivan had ascertained from his examination of the body *in situ* whether this was indeed death by natural causes, or if it needed further investigation, he would make a decision and the authorities would be informed. The latter would mean the body was removed with the Coroner's permission, an autopsy would ensue, and a murder investigation could open up. I sensed something was very wrong. Kendel might want us out of the way, and to hide whatever it was, but I hoped to dig deep using the time I had well.

'I have not determined if he died of natural causes yet, Hector.' He wagged a finger at me, then peered at eye-level with the victim. 'Although he does appear to have moved after death, which is more than a little suspicious,' he added, and smiled at me. 'He has been dead at least eight hours, I would say — possibly up to twelve.' Ivan was a man who loved his work. It was not a dead body to him; more akin to a puzzle to unravel. No matter if the cause was natural or not, a reason needed to be deduced and ascertained.

I looked at the bed; there were marks on the sheets and pillow as if they had been rubbed down. I sniffed. 'I would say he had been vomiting over this side.'

The blanket was wrapped between his legs, twisted around him. Ivan, meanwhile, was finishing looking at his face, hair, neck and hands.

'Leave me to explore further, I realise you have your keen policeman's nose to sniff out suspicious circumstances, but I would ask you to be patient. Whilst you see your witnesses and glean what information you can, I will see what is amiss up here, and hopefully we can wrap this one up quickly. If the man was drunk, and suffocated or choked on his own vomit, then it will be natural causes, Hector, and you and I can go home to our lovely wives. Otherwise . . . well, we shall see.'

He looked at me with what appeared to be doubt over the last statement. He would be thorough, and that was all I could ask of him.

'Take your time; look at every detail, Ivan. There is something here that I do sense is seriously amiss,' I admitted.

'Very well; but this is not an official investigation yet, so please be swift until it is or is not.' He smiled, but then winked at me. 'I shall be thorough, so you ask your questions quickly.'

I nodded and left him, making my way down to the study. I had my suspicions, but did not want to plant ideas in Ivan's head. He was a good man; I did not envy him his task, because I could bear police work, but witnessing a dissection was something that turned my stomach, no matter how much of the bleak side of mankind's crimes I had seen. There was something cold about it: the body was no longer human, a person; and that, I had trouble relating to. When a body was found, I wanted to know who had killed the person and stolen away their future. I was not, and never would be, able to see flesh and blood as a butcher looked upon a carcass. Yet Ivan had a good heart, and was the liveliest and most optimistic of men. He saw that, by using the evidence the corpse could reveal, detection could move further and quicker in a more accurate fashion than it had ever done before.

Meanwhile, I could focus on the living. One of them could know of some malicious intent against the dead man. One might know who would harm him, and why. And one of them might well be the murderer. I was becoming excited, which was not very professional. Was Kendel right? Did I secretly hope to make more of a young man's untimely death? A little, perhaps, but it was certainly more to get my teeth into than Ben Higgins' mystery of his chickens disappearing from their hutch.

In the last year, I knew that I was learning fast that to be a good detective one had to observe and listen; collect facts along with the fiction people told you, and then separate the two. Sometimes the obvious was the wrong solution, too easy to see and believe; at other times, the obvious was exactly the simplest and correct answer. Determining which was true in a case was deduced by reading people, and I was about to enjoy listening to them very shortly. First, I would share the news with Kendel that I was about to take up my seat of inquisition in his master's office, and he would bring each servant to me in turn, at my request. I smiled at the thought. After all, I am only human, and he had hurt so many in the past that to see him humble would be a long-awaited blessing.

3

My moment of reverie was soon to be cut short, as Ivy was already standing nervously before Mr Denton's desk when I entered the office. To my surprise, Kendel was just standing up from the man's chair, moving away in a calm manner. Mr Denton was barely cold, and this man was so keen to jump into his seat.

'I have already questioned the girl, Blagdon,' he said to me dismissively, making no attempt to leave. 'I will give you my notes, and you can leave.'

'You are the one who may go now. Please find Mrs Bellington, and have her ready to attend me when Ivy leaves after my interview with her.'

'If you must, but I should stay . . . ' He placed a fist down on the table and leaned toward me to stress his point. 'It is not proper for the girl to be left in here with you.'

'She was in here with you, and wanders into her employer's bedchamber of a morning, so your presence won't be necessary.' I held the door for him as he walked reluctantly out.

'Sit down, Ivy.' I watched her as she did. Her emotions had stilled, the bubbling temper I had seen earlier had settled, and she calmly but soberly sat opposite the desk. She did not seem at all disturbed by the exchange I had had with Kendel. I sat down in the dead man's chair and, using his pen and paper, scribbled *Ivy* and the time and date at the top of a sheet.

'What time did you find Mr Denton?' I asked, glancing up to catch her impassive expression.

'Seven forty-five a.m., sir.'

'Precisely?' I continued. Kendel had obviously asked her these straightforward questions, but I wanted her to feel comfortable, so when my less simple ones followed perhaps her answers would also.

'Yes, sir. The clock in the hall chimes at the quarter hour,' she explained. 'No one could miss it as it is so loud and the walls seemed to echo it up the stairs.'

'How was he when you found him?' I continued.

'Dead, sir,' came her short reply, and those cobalt pearls met mine as I looked away. They were now moist and somehow seemed quite desperate.

I cleared my throat, as I had not been succinct in the question, but when she said the word 'dead' her countenance had changed. 'I actually meant, how was he positioned on the bed when you found him? Tell me — from opening the door, what did you actually see?' I remembered her words from earlier when she had said he was 'staring'. How, if his face was in the pillow, could she see his eyes to know what they were doing? Either someone was lying and had moved the body, or this girl was wrong. Were they trying to make it look as though he had died naturally, suffocating himself in his pillow whilst in a drunken stupor? I intended to find out.

'I had the tray with his coffee on in my right hand, and the bucket for the fire in my left. I placed the drink tray on the carpet and pushed the door open. I dropped the bucket by the fire, hoping he would stir, as I didn't like to be in there whilst he was sleeping. If he was awake, then I could talk to him.' She looked away from me, and then swallowed. 'It may seem improper, but he liked to talk to me.'

I watched a delicate blush appear on her cheeks as she fought to continue.

'I turned to take him his coffee, and was going to give it to him when I noticed he wasn't moving at all, and his eyes . . .' she swallowed hard and fought to keep her composure.

'You saw his eyes?' I asked, not wanting to reveal why I ask this specifically. Yet, this simple statement had revealed so much already. I was certain she told the truth for the horror of the moment was relived in those beautiful, yet sad eyes.

'Yes, they were staring straight up,' she sniffed. 'I'll never forget them. Smaller somehow, yet more piercing. They were looking, yet could not see me or anything . . . I don't know if I dropped the coffee or tossed it in the air as I screamed, but then I ran, sir. I ran because Mr Denton, a man who had been so kind to me, was dead.' She looked down and sobbed, but then sniffed hard and raised her face again.

'Who was the first person you saw as you ran away?' I could tell she was becoming very emotional by her desperate fight to control her outburst, but I wanted to keep her talking to me calmly.

'Mr Kendel was crossing the bottom of the stairs. The old grandfather clock always needs adjusting each day, and he takes great care of it. It reminds him of Mr Denton Senior, he told me once when I was polishing it. Apparently the old man was good to him.'

'Who entered the room next?' I had no wish to share in Kendel's nostalgic ramblings. Why would anyone have been good to Kendel back in the days when he was such a brute? The old man had obviously lacked vision in his dotage, and misplaced his compassion.

'I don't know, sir. I went to the kitchens. I . . . I . . . needed a bucket . . . I was sick, sir.' She looked embarrassed, but I was familiar enough with the human condition that to consider this detail anything but a normal reaction would have been strange. In fact, I would have expected a young maid to still be feeling the effect of such a shock. This one, although shaken, somehow had inner strength to her.

'When I left the kitchens, you said that he had promised you something. To whom did you refer and what was promised to you?' I was pushing her now. I needed answers that would give me a lead as to what had happened in the last hours of Denton's life and why. She was holding something other than tears back, of that I was certain.

I watched as she licked her lips; they seemed dry. Her eyes watered, and she gripped the edge of her apron with her hands.

'Ivy, tell me, in confidence if you must, but I need to understand what has happened here, and I believe you are withholding evidence.' I felt cruel. I felt like a bully as those beautiful eyes widened and fear crossed her now-expressive face. I wanted the truth, and I would scare her into revealing it — gently, I hoped, if I could.

'I was not speaking sense, sir . . . I was shocked, and . . . ' She was backtracking.

'Do you know it is an offence to lie to an officer of the law, Ivy?' I stared at her as a brutal headmaster would at a child he was about to cane. I needed her to talk to me.

'But, I have no proof . . . ' Her voice was low.

'Proof of what?' I was intrigued. Had Denton tricked the poor lass into a clandestine affair? She would hardly be the first maid to fall for the owner of a fine manor house. The life of maids was hard and a pretty young lass like her would make a good life for herself if she could escape the daily grind. Or worse, could be used and turned out if she fell with child. Who would take her word against his? It was a well enough known scenario.

'Proof of what?' I waited impatiently, trying not to push so hard she folded, but nudging her to spill the secret.

'He was going to send me away.' She

looked down. 'I told you, I have no proof of it; but it won't happen now, so it makes no mind, does it?'

'Why, had you done something you perhaps shouldn't have?' I asked, wondering if she was in fact with child.

'No, sir.' She paused. I was surprised when her head shot up. 'Nothing like that. Mr Denton was a true gentleman.' Her chin lifted, those watery eyes betrayed what she truly felt; the girl was in love with him. Yet he had such a beautiful wife: infatuation, perhaps? 'I am a respectable young woman!' She was becoming slightly more agitated. I needed to move fast and finish this interview before she crumbled.

'Then explain what you mean and dispel my doubts, Ivy,' I persisted, more gentle in my tone this time.

'He was getting me a position, an interview in London, sir.' She looked at me beseechingly. 'He said I should be a lady's maid, and next time he went down town, as he called it, he would take me with him . . . It was tomorrow that we were going to go . . . I was just to dress up nice and take an overnight bag . . . only it won't be now . . . I'll never be going, will I? I'll be stuck here for years, scrubbing and cleaning and lighting fires before the sun rises in winter, and . . . ' Then her resolve did crumble and she cried like a child.

My eyes were truly opened. Her grief was genuine enough, but it was for the loss of a dream and not the death of her employer. How fickle the young heart was. 'Who were you to have the interview with?' I asked.

'A lady . . . a real lady!' she said proudly. 'I was going to meet people, see places and wear nice clothes. Who knows what could have happened?' She sniffed.

'No name?' I saw the lovelorn dreams of an infatuated girl, and wished I could explain what the reality would have most likely been like. She would have seen real people — especially a man, no doubt — and possibly more of the real world than her innocent mind could imagine. She had possibly been saved from ruination.

'No, sir, I didn't ask. But she lived near

Buckingham Palace, and was close to proper royalty.' She smiled and wiped the tears away with the back of her hand.

'You may go. Ask Mr Kendel to send in Mrs Bellington.' I looked at her: a beautiful, gullible girl who had much to learn in life about the lies men will tell her to have their way. I doubted the 'lady' ever existed.

'Yes, sir,' she replied, and took two steps away. 'Sir . . . '

'Yes, Ivy?' I replied as she sheepishly looked back at me, her fingers twisting the edge of her apron. It would need restarching after its treatment today.

'You won't tell Mr Kendel, will you? That I said aught . . . It was supposed to be our secret. You see, I was to leave like Millicent, and Mrs Bellington was fussed about having to train a new girl up so soon after settling Millie in.'

'Millicent?' I raised a brow. Who was Millicent, and where had this girl gone — to the mysterious lady?

'The lass who worked here before me. She left six months ago.' Ivy shrugged.

'Did she have an interview for a

position as a lady's maid too?' I was curious. I knew that the turnover of servants in the cities was high, but here positions were not so readily available, and neither was there a steady flow of young girls to fill them. This seemed a distraction from the matter of Mr Denton's death, yet it instantly struck a nerve, a pointer that something else was amiss here.

'No, sir, she ran off with a lad from the village. Tommy had a good heart, but he was just a village lad with limited prospects.' She sniffed. 'He was a simple farmhand, you see. He had an eye for her, always had. He would be lurking around the lane on laundry day in the hope he would see her as she hung out the sheets.' She smiled. 'Now, there was a girl who behaved badly and did things she shouldn't of, and she paid the consequences for it, no doubt.' She tried to look justifiably wise, her nose ever so slightly raised aloft. The little fool, I thought. At least this Millie had had a man to look after her.

That little chin of hers tilted up, and I

could not help but think how it could have been so cruelly lowered if she had gone with Denton to London. What sort of a kind-hearted master would he have been proved to be? Or was I becoming a cynical policeman?

'Well, Ivy, I am here just to ascertain facts, not share gossip or tales of lost promises made to impressionable young girls.'

She smiled. My patronising words brought a glint of annoyance to her pretty eyes. 'Thank you, sir.' She walked to the door.

I stared at her straight back as I mulled over the few facts I had learnt. Denton was on his back when she entered his room. The man obviously had a soft spot for her — or had he more of a desire for her, and so sought to entrap her in some way? I thought of the delectable Mrs Amelia Grace Denton and felt sorry for her if that was the kind of man he had been. He already had a charming wife . . .

Ivy left, and Kendel entered without being asked. I made my notes before acknowledging him. When our eyes met, he showed open anger.

'Is Mrs Bellington ready?' I looked behind him with an equally stern countenance.

'Yes.' He approached the desk. 'She is a tender soul, so be kinder to her than you obviously were to young Ivy. She has been most distressed by this unfortunate natural occurrence, and all this tomfoolery is making it more difficult for her and us all. This is not a murder investigation, man! When I find out who dared to use the house telephone without my permission, and summon you as if this was some common murder hunt, I will . . . ' His fists were clenched at his side, and I remembered the young lad he had been when those same fists, unrestrained, would fly freely into his next prey. In a way, I longed for him to try it, for I would floor the man as easily as I had then. I was fit: I cycled, walked, and ran up hills. He swaggered around a Hall, and ate his fill in the kitchens with extras from Cook.

I was not inclined to share my recent knowledge that it was Ivy's lost opportunity to live a better life away from his domain that grieved her so, and not specifically Mr Denton's death. The momentary silence was broken by an unexpected confession.

'It was me, Mr Kendel. I took it upon myself to call in the police.' The tired voice came from a slight figure standing in the open doorway. 'I telephoned the police station, Mr Kendel,' she repeated clearly, and looked at me. 'I am Mrs Bellington.' She introduced herself confidently enough for someone who had been 'most distressed' not so long before. Although, from the blotches on her complexion and reddened nose, I could see plainly that she had indeed been crying.

'Why did you not ask me, Ethel ... Mrs Bellington?' Kendel asked, clearly surprised by her admission. 'This is most irregular; you should have come to me. I would have known what to do.' He looked taken aback, which was most intriguing.

'Because I simply acted on instinct as I felt I must, Mr Kendel.' Her eyes bore into mine as if she was trying to convey a sense of urgency or purpose; she did not look at him. 'I never meant to undermine your position, Mr Kendel; but it was so sudden, and I felt . . . '

'Thank you, Mr Kendel. Please leave us now, and I will bear your advice in mind. If you could tell Cook that I will speak with her next, I would be most grateful.' I looked at him, smiled politely, and raised an eyebrow; he dared not challenge me again. This small-framed woman seemed to have taken the wind out of his sails. Somehow he left the room a smaller man than the one who had entered.

4

'Please take a seat, Mrs Bellington,' I said as she approached the desk.

She was dressed in a dark navy dress that flattered her petite figure. Her coppery hair was swept up into a neat bun. Odd wisps were loose, but she held her poise well, sitting straight-backed, hands cupping each other on her lap. She was a good few years younger than I had expected.

'What did your instincts tell you, Mrs Bellington?' I cut straight to the quick. I wanted to ascertain the household situation before the good doctor finished his work. Also, before any complaint that Kendel could make had a chance to result in anyone asking questions of me.

'My instincts told me that it was not natural.' She seemed calm and fully committed to her observations of the situation.

'What was not natural?' I asked.

'His body; the way he was. His death; he was so young and strong. His sudden turn from good health to bad.' She blinked before continuing. 'I have tended the weak and ailing, sir. He was violently sick in the early hours of the morning; it came on suddenly, then he was calm, too still. When I entered the room, he was just staring up at the ceiling and quite lifeless. I do not think he passed easily.' She swallowed, and regained her composure.

'When did you enter the room?' I was intrigued. She too had seen him staring upward.

'I entered the room just after Ivy ran down the stairs screaming for Mr Kendel. I went straight along the landing from my bedchamber. You see, Mrs Denton's room is adjoined to Mr Denton's by a door, and I sleep in the servant's room off hers. She can have spells of panic during the night, and it suits her to have me there to call upon as comfort when they occasionally occur. Bartholomew . . . Mr Denton was just laid there. In my heart, I knew he had passed on, but I had to do something . . . so I rolled him onto his front and tried to push breath into him. I had seen it done once with a child who was choking. It worked then, but Mr Denton was gone already, I was too late.' She looked down at her hands nestled in her lap before clearing her throat and staring back at me.

'What did you do next?' I was amazed at this slight woman's practicality, and ability to think and act calmly in such a life-and-death situation. Yet again, a person seemed sad at the passing of Mr Denton, but I wondered if there was another reason behind her emotions. Surely, as she had a good position, it could not be the loss of opportunity as it had been in Ivy's case.

'I could do nothing, and so I ran back to my room. I . . . was upset.' She bit her bottom lip and fought to control herself. 'I heard Mr Kendel's voice. I was in my nightdress, and there was no more I could do for Mr Denton, so I left by going back through Mrs Denton's room to my own. She was sleeping soundly, totally undisturbed by all the commotion.'

'Is there a Mr Bellington?' I asked, and changed my line of questioning to help her think clearly again. It worked; she sniffed and half-smiled at my question. Then she laughed; the sound was somehow hollow. 'Pardon; no, there is no Mr Bellington. It is thought respectable to be called 'Mrs' as I am a housekeeper.'

She almost looked annoyed. I was familiar with this custom, but I had wondered, as there was no reason she could not have been a young widow herself. It would explain how she came to such a position at an earlier age than most. 'Mrs Bellington, you are quite young, are you not, for such a position?'

'I suppose that depends on the observer's perspective. To you, I am young; to a child, I am old; and to the world, I am and will be seen as an old spinster with no marriageable prospects.' Her eyes hardened somehow.

There was a note of arrogance in her words; such a contrast. I waited for her to tell me her age. When I did not challenge her comments, or comment upon them, she continued.

'I am twenty-seven, sir.' She half-smiled. 'Mr Denton did not want a dour housekeeper, although a more mature butler is essential, apparently.' Her eyes sparkled; they were tired, red from her upset, but something within them shone brightly — or, rather, defiantly.

'So I ask again, what did your instinct tell you?' I had her back on track, and she did not disappoint.

'Just that it was not natural — and, if that was true, then there was need for the police to be here quickly.'

'Why did you not go to Mr Kendel first? Did Mr Denton have enemies?' I asked.

'Because he would have thought of the family's name rather than what should happen. Mr Denton was charming. He was most attentive to his estate and household . . . and yet, yes, I think he had. He was a man who knew what he wanted and would do everything in his power to have it. Mr Denton had a certain way with him. He liked money and was quite able to spend it.'

Her stare was most direct. Her words were so bold. Her hair had the colour of fire flecked within it, and her answers held the same spark. This lady was astute, and again I sensed an undertone of anger.

'He had plenty to spend, though, so why not?' I observed the furnishings around me and the gold pen-stand upon his desk. To have so much seemed a blessing from my viewpoint, as we had always had so little.

'Yes, he did. He had his father's money inherited, and then his wife's fortune to whittle away — and he happily did so, as was his legal right.' Her mouth set in a firm line.

I did not comment upon this last revelation. It implied he had had motive to marry, and was incompetent with his acquired wealth. What was it they called the love of money — the root of all evil?

'Who within this household might want to harm him?' I enquired, suspecting that Mrs Bellington's reply might indeed be more direct and informative than Ivy's.

'I do not point fingers,' she said quickly. I was disappointed.

'Miss . . . Mrs Bellington, this is not a game. This is a man's life taken or expired in his prime, and if it was indeed unnatural, then someone has to have been close enough to him to arrange his demise.' Both my hands were placed palms-down on the desk as I continued to look at her. I had every respect for an intelligent woman, but would not be toyed with by anyone.

She looked towards the door and lowered her voice. 'He behaved badly to Mr Kendel at times. He made fun of him in front of the young maids, and that is unforgivable. Mr Denton's humour was often cruel. He teased his wife endlessly, he poked fun at people who were not in a position to answer back. Mrs Denton's nerves have not been good as a result, and now the poor woman is so drugged that she hardly knows the day of the week — well, some days, at least. Others, she is fine. It depends on if she takes her medication. I fear for her well-being, as she is not strong in worldly terms.' Her words were spoken quietly, but the softness of the last statement revealed her admiration for her mistress, or her pity. It was as if she felt her to be vulnerable, and perhaps wondered how the woman would cope now she was a widow — albeit a very rich one, perhaps, unless her late husband owed debtors. I, too, felt fond of Mrs Amelia Grace Denton and was anxious to see her again. I wondered if I could get Ivan to examine her as well. He would be able to look at her 'medication' and see if it was appropriate or needed.

'Would Mr Kendel wish him harm?' I asked outright. I wanted to witness her reaction: shock, denial, or confrontation.

'Perhaps, but he would not hurt the man. He was under his charm. He'd do anything for Mr Denton.' She looked down again as if her eyes would betray some secret.

Interesting, I thought. Why would Kendel be charmed by a younger gentleman . . . one who teased him? An uncomfortable thought crossed my mind. I shifted my weight in the chair as I pondered how to broach it.

I cleared my throat. 'When you say that Mr Kendel was charmed by Mr Denton, do you imply that . . . he was attracted to the man in an . . . unhealthy way . . . obsessed..?' My words were lost to me. What I was about to ask was hardly fitting for this young woman's ears. She might not even be familiar with the possibility that two men could establish an attraction akin to a courting couple. However, women can often wrongfoot a man, and Mrs Bellington was no exception. She laughed at my unease.

'Heavens, no, sir. I did not mean to imply any such kind of . . . relationship. Mr Kendel is most definitely a man who would be wed if a woman was foolhardy enough to fall for him.' She breathed in deeply to control herself. 'I simply meant that he admired the man's poise, position and power. Mr Denton could charm anyone when he had a mind to . . . until they began to know him better. You see, he liked to control people. Some men are like that; they want to dominate anyone in their service. It is rather like being a god in their own world. However, this god gave no one free will.' She looked directly at me, and I could only admire her clarity of vision and her way of expressing it in kind.

'Has Mr Kendel asked you to marry

him, Ethel?' I deliberately used her Christian name as Kendel had.

She smiled, as he had let her name slip when he had been so affronted by her taking such a decision as to act without consulting him and phone the police station.

'Yes, he has.' She said no more.

'Did you agree?' I asked, doubting she had but wondering what reason she would give for not being fool enough to marry the man.

'No, I haven't. You see, he does not understand that I have a mind of my own.' She smiled after saying these bold words, and I could clearly see that she did.

'Are you a member of the Suffragette movement?' I was sensing a soul who sought her own power.

'I admire the Suffragettes, but I would hardly be a housekeeper if I was a militant or anarchist. I seek to live in a fair society, but I do not wish to damage any part of it. I just want women to have a voice of their own and to be respected as equal to a man.' Her voice had calmed again. Her emotions were back under control. That clarity of vision, I feared, extended far into the future, because what she sought would not be granted her in our lifetimes. I was certain of that.

'Did the Dentons know this?'

She shook her head. 'No, they would have turned me out on the street if they had. Any threat to the status quo of rank, position, and male domination would have been seen as almost heretical in their eyes.' She shook her head. 'They have no idea how people, women in particular, suffer daily.'

'And you have?' I asked.

'I have seen and helped the poor and lived among them. My father was a missionary,' she admitted.

'But you do not wish to convert new souls?'

'I wish to see their flesh fed, their rights recognised, and their souls saved — in that order.'

'Why risk telling me, then, that you hold these views?' I was genuinely curious.

'Instinct!' she simply said.

'Were you here when Millicent left?' I did not know why I asked, as this was a sidestep from the investigation, but somehow I trusted this woman — and she, apparently, did me.

She nodded. 'Yes, the girl — pretty, she was — supposedly ran off with a lad from the village.'

'Supposedly? Is this instinct talking again?' I leant my chin on my interlocked fingers as I rested my elbows on the desk.

'No, I listened to gossip. You see, Tommy's mother was in the grocer's in the village when I popped in, and she was saying how he had been found work in London. Millicent had apparently gone with him and was also working there, but he hadn't said as what. However, he was hoping to return next summer and marry a girl called Sarah. She was from Beckton Hall over Gorebeck way. Last word she had from him was that he was serving as a footman and doing well in a rich man's house. I heard no more as the queue moved on.'

I wrote down the name of Tommy's mother, and her address.

'Is Ivy a local girl?' I asked. This was becoming more curious than the questions about Mr Denton's last hours.

'She was brought in from an orphanage in a town over the moor, near Whitby. Millicent was from another one in Beckton Dale. Young Annie, the scullery maid, was brought here last week from the same orphanage as Millicent. She is only thirteen. If they have no family, they are less likely to be distracted or drift off, I am told. That is at least what Mr Kendel explained to me; but in the year I have been here, three have left already and been replaced.' She sighed. 'It's a strange household to work for.'

'Domestics are difficult to get and keep these days. Where did you arrive from?' I continued, but even I thought three maids having departed was high. Perhaps not in London, but this was the North Riding of Yorkshire.

'I, sir, came with Mrs Denton. I was her personal maid, and when the position of housekeeper came free, my mistress insisted I was appointed. It was a surprise to me, but I could hardly say no as it was a promotion. After all, I can hardly profess to think women should be given more opportunities, and then turn down a promotion at — as you say — such a young age. I can only assume she thought my skills worthy of the position, and I respect that trust.'

'Who did you replace?' I queried, wondering if their turnover of housekeepers was also quick.

'Mrs Tibbet; she retired.'

No mystery there, then, I thought. 'Your instinct isn't telling you any more about who would wish Mr Denton harm if they had the chance, then?' I picked up my initial line of questioning.

She shook her head. 'I know no more, but if I have wasted your time, then I apologise. If I have not, then . . . ' She stared directly at me. She seemed as if she was almost willing to tell me more, but had drawn a line that I suspected she would not cross.

'Take care, Mrs Bellington. Please ask Mr Kendel to send in the cook as soon as possible.' I had finished asking her my questions for now.

She stood up and nodded. 'I am not a fanciful woman by nature, sir. I believe a wrong has been done here, but it is not for an individual to bring a man to judgement and offer sentence. And when the man has so much power on his side, would the police listen to an accusation from, say, a young girl or a single woman in service?' Her head was gently tilted to one side.

I wanted plain talking and not oblique gestures. 'If you wish to be more explicit, Mrs Bellington, then sit down again. Otherwise, please be about your duties after you have sent in Cook. I have no time to entertain riddles.' I deliberately snapped at her. I was not sure why, except that time was ticking by. Was Kendel hiding a dark secret that she felt torn loyalties about revealing? Was he annoyed by his spurned feelings, or by his master's sarcasm to him, and had revisited his old violent ways? Was Ivy in danger of being duped? What was it this woman before me was alluding to?

She left without further word. I watched her go, and wondered if she meant that Ivy had cause to hate the man. If so, why would the girl have shared with me about his promise? No one would know of it, and hardly anyone other than me would believe it. But I too had instincts.

5

Kendel blundered into the office. Mrs Elmwood followed behind him. Something was bothering her, and although she strove to hide her feelings, the glistening eyes betrayed her thoughts. The cook had a naturally ruddy complexion, no doubt from years of leaning over fires and a hot stove, and her short, stocky appearance seemed determined in stride and strong of body. I sensed that she was not grieving very deeply for Mr Denton, but why? In appearance, she looked well-fed and healthy. No suffering there, then.

'Thank you, Kendel. Please close the door as you leave.' My mood had darkened and my manner with it. Patience towards Kendel was running thin.

He did, with more efficiency than needed. The bang brought a chuckle from the cook, which I ignored.

'When did you see Mr Denton last?' I began to ask.

'Yesterday. He had been drinking after dinner, and I slipped out of the servants' stairs near the hallway to go into the library and see if Mrs Bellington was finished with her tray. Normally one of the girls would fetch it, but as I wanted to see her about the menus for next week, I thought I could have a word and save us both time. He was just going up the stairs. Said as he didn't feel right and was retiring early. He had a bottle of his medicine in his hands; no glass needed, as he swilled it down as he went . . . best brandy, it was. The man had a thirst for drink that would champion the best sailor in the docks after months at sea,' she said, and chuckled again. It was not far removed, I thought, from dancing a jig on a dead man's grave. I did not approve, but wondered why her loyalty to her master was not troubled as others was.

'Are you familiar with many docks and sailors, Mrs Elmwood?' I asked dryly. I did not care for her blunt manner, even if she did not respect the man who had paid her wages.

'Saucy one you are, then. No, I'm not,

but I've lived on this earth long enough not to be green like these young lasses that gets brought in.' Her tone changed. 'I have kept my eyes open, but have had to keep me mouth firm shut. But you is here now, and so this is me chance to speak as I find, isn't it?'

'Brought in?' I repeated, not answering her direct question. Each woman I interviewed seemingly had a tale of their own to tell or a different concern to air.

'Aye. Lizzie, Sally, Bethany, Millicent, Ivy, young Sarah. All brought here from orphanages, as if in an act of charity . . . but you tell me how it is that they are all pretty and all disappear — an aunt suddenly needed her after tracing Bethany down, the family now out of poor circumstance. Sally, dismissed when I'm not even told until after she'd gone, and why? Fooling around with a farmhand, they said — gone, and no one is told where. Her name not to be mentioned. So what am I to think, and . . . what was it you were asking?' She had lost her train of thought completely as she had been so intent on putting her own concerns over to me.

'You seem to want to tell me something. What is it you are implying?' I could be as blunt as her, but would she move forward from her questions to direct accusations.

'Me? Implying? No, sir, not me. I'm just pointing out that what a coincidence it is that young girls come and go from here, like at quite regular intervals, and us such a backwater nowhere near the city.' She deliberately smacked her lips closed, emphasising the gesture.

'Do you feel that these 'coincidences' have any connection to the death of Mr Denton?' I tried to connect the two lines of investigation, for now it seemed I had missing persons to track down too. I must see if they were merely being trained up and moved on at a profit, or discover what else had happened to them.

She looked around her, a little flustered for a moment. This woman seemed straightforward and honest, but not able to think things through clearly. Or was she scared of someone discovering what she had been saying — and, if so, did the finger point at Kendel?

'How would I know that?' She stared back at me, then leaned forward and said in a lower voice, 'You saying he was murdered, right here in his own bed? I thought he drank himself stupid and choked on his own vomit. How else, then?' She shrugged. 'It was the way he behaved, not really like a gentleman at all.'

'No, I'm not saying that at all. I am trying to provide a report to support the doctor's when he has finished his examination, to ascertain the events surrounding Mr Denton's last hours.' She might be more worldly then the young maids she saw come and go, but I knew for a fact that his behaviour was quite common amongst 'gentlemen'.

'Well, I don't know about that, but I do know there is no one to stand up for the girls. They have no folks, and I just thought how, as you were a detective man, you might be able to trace a few and see they is all right. There is no one to speak out for them. They have no family, sir.' She looked hopefully at me. 'I need to know, for I cannot sleep some nights for wondering about them. They are as lost souls with no one to look over them.' Her face was serious; she felt for them. And, surprisingly, I felt for her. I had got her message clearly enough. She seemed not to care for Mr Denton, but had a burning desire to know what had happened to the girls who had passed through the estate.

Her bottom lip protruded slightly. Her eyes did not moisten with emotion, but they were kind, warm ones, and I felt I would have to look into her concerns. There was no motive behind her request but care, which I respected.

'You are asking me to investigate the whereabouts of the girls with no knowledge of why, just that you want to know where they are. Is that correct?'

'Wasting me breath, aren't I? Who cares, eh, what happens to single young lasses on their own in this world?' She stood up.

'Sit back down ... please, Mrs Elmwood.' I changed the tone of my voice. She was right. No one would take her concerns seriously, as the owner of the estate had provided a reason or explanation for their absence.

I pulled a piece of paper from the drawer and gave her a pencil. 'You write down their names, the places they came from, when they left, and the reason they left.'

'You'll look, then?' she said optimistically.

'I will,' I replied.

She smiled at that and eagerly picked up the pencil.

'Sorry I snapped at you, sir,' she muttered as she wrote away, taking care to use her best writing with pride.

'You cared about them all?' I said, matter-of-factly.

'I was a lass from a poorhouse. I learnt how to look out for myself, and when I got the chance to work in a big house I grabbed it. I slaved away for a cook in a warm kitchen with food aplenty, and I swore I'd not know cold or hunger again. Then, when I moved here and became Cook, I promised that I'd help me kitchen or scullery maids to learn their way to a better life. But they never stay long enough. And that's just not right. I

74

can feel it in me bones.'

'Ivy is very upset.' I wondered if she knew why. I was trying to probe just a little to see what her take on the girl's situation was.

Mrs Elmwood placed the pencil down and sat back. 'Aye, she took it right bad. Mind, she has not found a dead body before. Your first is always the worst. It's when it is brought home to you that the spirit has flown; that the shell, so to speak, is left. But also, she shouldn't have been going into a drunken man's bedroom on her own. It's just not right. I mean, what if he'd been using the pot or something? Not right,' she said, and shook her head to stress her point. 'However, Mr Kendel said it was because Mr Denton liked to see a pretty face first thing with his morning drink, as if that made it alright. Well, in my book it don't. What about Mrs Denton, poor thing? She was so very lovely. It should be *her* face he sees first thing. She was so full of life; now she is so poker-faced and dour. Like the fun left her heart.'

'Is there anything else you'd like to tell

me?' I asked gently, and glanced at the list. Her writing was clear enough; taking the information in, it did seem as though for these orphans, maids in training, there was a definite pattern being established.

She thought for a moment and wrung her hands. 'Ivy's a good lass. I don't want you thinking ill of her,' she said as she rose. 'I mean, I am sure nothing untoward has happened in his room. It is just, a man in his prime and out of his senses could get confused.'

'Why would I think that it had?' I asked, curious to know what she meant and why, other than her suggestions of impropriety.

'She sometimes lets her mouth run away with her, that's all.' She licked her lips and I noticed her hands were clamped together. Was there a tremble there I had missed?

'Did she confide in you, Mrs Elm-wood?' I wondered if this woman knew what was being arranged. 'Did she tell you, perhaps, of her plans for the future, if she had any?'

'Ivy is always full of fanciful notions.

She'd do well to find herself a good husband who could look after her and value her for more than her pretty eyes and looks. Still, we all had dreams when we were young.' She had sidestepped my question, and her confidence returned.

I thought of the irony in her words, for here was a woman who knew all too well when to let her tongue loose. We did all have dreams when we were young; mine were to join the force, stay away from the mines, and to have a happy home with a loving wife and children. That made me realise that I had achieved all but the last bit, for the children were still to come. One day they would, I hoped, for my Elsie had so much love to give. I was truly blessed with her, and she needed to be with young ones to care for when I was out long hours. To be truthful, until I had met Mrs Amelia Grace Denton the previous summer, I thought that my Elsie was perfect.

Stunned by my own musings, I watched the cook leave the room. She had seized the opportunity to have her concerns taken into account, even if it meant jumping in on a possible murder investigation. It was time to see Ivan again and find out what he had discovered. I had apparently uncovered a can of worms, but had no idea why Mr Denton had died.

I walked past Kendel, who lingered at the door. 'I will interview you shortly.' I went to continue up the stairs.

Ignoring his grunt, I continued ascending the richly carpeted stairs. This modest manor house was definitely well kept. The walls were hung with the pictures of the ancestors — whose did not matter, for Denton owned them now; or, rather, he had purchased their images for show.

The wood of the bannister, dark and gleaming, had been carved to perfection. I ran my hand over it. I have always loved the feel of perfectly polished old oak.

'Don't get ideas above your station, Blagdon. You won't be here for long.' Kendel's voice held its old bitter twist as he snapped his words of warning out at me. I merely stared down at him.

Then, patience wearing thin, I took a step back down, not quite lowering myself to his level — but then, I never had. I leaned over the handrail to face him above his eyeline. 'You should not tempt fate, man. For how long do you think you will be here serving a master who no longer exists? What use is a butler-cum-valet without a master to serve?' I had held my tongue long enough; my temper, I would have to hold longer, as I was in uniform and that gave me boundaries that I had to respect. Common brawling for old grudges was not considered justifiable or worthy of a man trusted to uphold the law.

'I have experience. I will be much sought-after. Mr Denton has friends in London. When they hear that a butler of good standing is without position, I shall be found employment in a house of status. I shall find decent work, Blagdon, and it won't be being dressed up like a bluebird plodding around the country after lowlifes.' He gave a cursory glance at my new uniform. I wore it proudly.

'Really, and who would these friends of his be?' I asked. So, he knew some of Denton's town associates.

He stood back, as if realising his words had run away with him. 'That is no concern of yours.' He briskly walked away.

6

I entered the bedchamber to see that Ivan had finished, and was packing up his bag and replacing his coat.

'Well, what do you think? Do you have conclusive answers for me?' I asked eagerly.

'The body has definitely been moved after death. From his posture, it looks as though he was manhandled onto his front. From the cadaveric rigidity, I would say that death occurred some hours before. His hands were clenched, gripping the sheet. His expression is not pleasant. I believe he was asphyxiated.' He stepped back, surveying the scene.

'Someone strangled or suffocated him?' I looked at the covered corpse and then at the door. Had I just preliminarily interviewed a murderer? It was an interesting thought — but who? I actually felt like I wanted this to be true. Was I so desperate to get my teeth onto a real detective case that I would wish a seemingly innocent servant to be a murderer?

'Well, there is no indentation in a discarded cushion or pillow that would fit with this type of assault. From the mess I was left with, I could not determine if there was a struggle, as the bed was so dishevelled. I would think not, as he had already partaken of a quantity of brandy. The pot has been emptied and cleaned, so I have not studied his . . . '

'That's a shame,' I cut in. I was not interested in the gory detail, just the conclusion. 'So, where are you going on this?' I asked, glad to be spared any more details.

'I am going to request that the body is removed for post-mortem investigation, and I would advise you to continue with your enquiries here.' He packed away his things.

'That is it?' I said, slightly downcast.

He smiled at me. 'Yes, but continue questioning; for I am not happy that this was natural causes, and I do not intend to say more.'

This, I knew, was near to him telling me he suspected murder outright, as he would not say before further examination was completed. But it was as good as fact. 'I will telephone the authorities and see that nothing is further disturbed, and will also make arrangements for the body's removal.' I was pleased that there was a strong possibility my senses were guiding me correctly.

'As soon as the permission is given, I will continue this investigation in greater detail. Take care, though. All is not straightforward here.'

I was beginning to realise just how true that statement was.

'Would you take a look at Mrs Denton whilst you are here?' I saw him look over his glasses at me as he picked up his bag. It was a look that told me I was pushing borders here; namely, the one that he should not cross.

'Has she requested to be seen by a doctor, Hector?' He raised an eyebrow, questioning my motive.

I shrugged my shoulders. 'Not exactly, but her ex-maid, the now-housekeeper, has raised concerns about her medication. To be truthful I cannot believe such a vibrant lady of a year ago can have slipped so low without good reason. Ailment or medication may be the cause, but I would know which for certain.' I tried not to give even the slightest inclination that I found her appealing a year ago.

'We are going beyond our duty here, Hector. However, yes I will, but only if you can use that silver tongue of yours to gain me access downstairs. I would like to see the kitchens also. Do you think we could arrange it without raising any suspicions?' He raised both eyebrows, knowing fine well I would find a way.

'Of course, Ivan. All things are possible when dealing with an overpuffed buffoon of a butler. Why anyone wants someone handy with his fists as their 'man', I do not know.' I paused, having vented my feelings slightly. 'Very well, I will please Kendel further by commandeering the use of the telephone to get things moving. He will be delighted. However, do look for any sign of abuse in any form, Ivan, when you see Mrs Denton. I care not for what I have learnt of the man so far — Mr Denton, that is — so let's be thorough.' I had no proof of any wrongdoing, yet this Denton man had had some bad and strange habits. He drank to excess, and preferred seeing young girls on waking. He might be dead, but I did not like him.

'When am I anything but discreet?' he said. 'But I can hardly give the woman a complete examination. However, I will look at her neck and any visible skin for signs of bruising.' He looked around the room, then added, 'This is highly irregular, Hector. Also, when men hurt their wives in such a fashion, they are usually careful not to leave marks that can be seen. These women need to be able to appear in public and function as if all was well. Basically, men who hit women are cowards who do not want the world to know their perverse secret.'

I nodded, because he was a true friend, and I knew him to be a thoroughly decent chap. The type of man he described was sadly common enough. Women stayed with them because they were trapped by lack of money, the needs of their children; or, in some strange cases, a sense of loyalty to the man. I had come across one such couple that mystified me. The husband had convinced the woman that all was her fault.

Still, I had Elsie, and I would never hurt her. I might have my fantasy about Mrs Amelia Grace, but that was all it was — a flight of fancy in an otherwise routine life.

'I owe you, Ivan,' I said. He seemed content that I had acknowledged this debt. I was more than content that he would do his damnedest to help solve the mystery here.

7

As we left the room, Kendel was hovering at the top of the stairs. 'Could you fetch Mrs Bellington?' I asked him, but neither of us was in any doubt that it was another order and I expected his immediate compliance.

'You have spoken to her already!' he snapped.

'Can you fetch her, man?' I repeated, and stared at him as he glared back at me.

'Is that an official command, Blagdon, or do you just want a cup of tea? If so, you can go to the kitchens and ask Cook.'

'Bring her, and stop wasting my time!' I raised my voice, and was surprised when the lady was duly brought out of her room.

'Could you please show Dr Jackman to see Mrs Denton, Mrs Bellington?' I gestured politely towards Mrs Denton's room door. 'I think it would be advisable that a doctor be there when she stirred.'

'Yes, sir,' she replied, and motioned for him to join her without question.

'Good, good. Now, Kendel, if you could take me to the telephone, I have some calls to make and arrangements to see to.' I forced a polite smile onto my face in an attempt to break the perpetual tension between us.

I saw Ivan also smile pleasantly at the lady as he followed her into the next bedchamber. Meanwhile, I returned to the hallway.

'I can make arrangements from here on in, as the doctor has finally finished,' Kendel barked.

He tried to pass me on the stairs to arrive at the study ahead of me, but I was fitter from all my 'plodding' than he was, so it was my hand that opened the door first.

'The doctor has finished here . . . yes.' His shoulders straightened as if to say *I told you so*. Then I added, 'But his business is far from concluded. An autopsy will be requested — a post-mortem. The doctor needs to be certain of the course of death. It is his job and duty to make sure that nothing untoward is being missed here. I therefore officially order you to make sure that no one should enter that room, and inform you that there will be further investigation as to the circumstances of Mr Denton's death. Dr Jackman is far from satisfied with the preliminary examination he has been able to complete here. Please tell the staff they must not leave the building until I have completed my . . . '

'Detecting!' he snapped.

'Exactly.' I walked into the study and closed the door behind me.

'You're wasting your time!' he bellowed through the door.

I ignored him. Instead, I revelled in the moment of having such an office and device to myself. How marvellous an invention the telephone was. I loved the idea that so much could be done in such a short time, instead of messages going across county by relay on bike or horse. I found inventions fascinating, and dreamed of the day when I could have such an amazing contraption in my own home. If only! Perhaps I could start a new dream to fulfil; the idea pleased me greatly. A man needed a goal in life, and I was still far too young to feel complete satisfaction at hitting my original ones. It was time to set some more — more ambitious ones, perhaps.

Once connected to the person at the other end of the line, I went through the adjustment of listening to a distant voice repeat my instructions in what sounded like a storm, talking or shouting against the wind. I still found it amazing to behold that we could communicate this way when I thought of how many miles were between us. When, several clicks later, the formalities of securing the Coroner's authority for the body to be removed to a place where further investigation could take place had been obtained, I looked at the other issue and decided to proceed. The detail of Ivan's work sometimes turned my stomach, as the stench of dissection was worse than that of freshly butchered meat, but it was also new and exciting at the same time. The world of clinical detection was growing: new methods, greater under-standing, and everything moving at a quickening speed.

I glanced down and saw the pencilled list that Cook had made. 'I would also like to track down the whereabouts of the following young women,' I said, and gave over the details, deciding that I might as well turn over more than one stone at a time here. Though if we did not discover the facts ourselves, then Scotland Yard would become involved, build a case on my suspicions, and no doubt take the credit for our local policing. Well, that might yet happen; but whilst I had the freedom to nose around and do some of my own detecting, I was going to make the most of it.

I leaned back in the leather chair and finished the telephone call. It was tempting to stay there and imagine being lord of the manor, but I had a lot of work yet to do, and time was running out. The early demise of my father and brother had taught me that time was my most prized commodity — precious to me, and never to be wasted.

However, curiosity got the better of me; I pulled open the desk drawer to my right, nosed around, and then did the same with the one to my left. Neither gave away anything of interest, just the usual desk contents: bits of stationery, pencils, rubber, nibs, ink. The other had sheets of headed notepaper. I was interested in furniture, though, as Elsie's father had been a carpenter in a local workshop, and told me fantastic tales of cabinets that had hidden drawers. He served his apprenticeship in a firm in London who made such pieces, and had done for nearly two hundred years, and this knowledge I had gleaned from him had helped me find many a hidden compartment.

There were decorative dowels down the side of the set of three drawers at each side. I felt the ones on the right, and they were rigid. However, sure enough, the ones on the left moved. I slid them away. The block of three drawers slipped out. I was suspicious because each drawer on that side contained only a few papers, meaning their weight was light and easier to manoeuvre. These drawers did not go the depth of the space. Behind, when touched lightly with the fingers, the panel at the back gave and dropped down to become a drawer itself. I had seized the moment and found that curiosity, in this instance, was its own reward.

This one proved no real test, although I was disappointed that I had not uncovered a blackmail note or hidden funds, or something more incriminating than half a dozen photographs of young women. They were scantily clad, except one respectable photograph of a lass looking pretty in a summery day dress. I wondered what she would think if she saw where he kept her image — along with the others, thrown into a plain brown envelope. Who was she?

I shook my head in disgust. The way the pictures were hidden suggested that their presence was not for an innocent purpose. Oh, I was no prude about the female form, I admired it greatly — but why should a man with a wife such as Mrs Amelia Grace Denton still need this sort of dross for his self-satisfaction? The thinking was beyond my understanding. Photography should capture the beauty of nature, but these images stole the girls' innocence. Their eyes were somehow aged beyond their years. Except, that is, for the girl in the dress.

Flicking them over, I saw that only the one that was respectably produced bore a mark, that of a Victor Braham of London. No doubt the pictures were sold in the 'gentlemen's clubs' that Denton belonged to. Looking further, I also uncovered a door key and a fob with the number 21 on it. Now my curiosity was definitely aroused. I began going through correspondence in the lower drawers, and quite forgot about time. It was only when my stomach growled that I remembered Ivan still wanted to see the kitchens.

There was a couple of bills left there that I wanted to investigate further. One was to a private members' club in St James, London. That would be one for the Yard, because they would not like a local detective ruffling the feathers of the well-heeled of the city. Besides, just being a member of a private club was hardly a crime; nor was simply owning photographs of barely-dressed young women, even if they were bordering on indecent. The other bill was a payment made for a quarterly rental to a property firm in Harrogate. Who and what Denton's affiliates were in Harrogate, I did not know, but I could find out.

I slipped the key into my pocket and returned the now-empty drawer to its previously hidden position. I made sure that the main drawers and the dowels were replaced properly so that my intrusion was not obvious. My brain was whirring with possibilities as to why they were there.

8

I left the office and met Ivan as he descended the stairs. 'You must be hungry,' I said in a bold voice, deliberately wanting it to be overheard by the maid who passed and slipped down the corridor before us.

'Well . . . ' He smiled. ' . . . now you ask, yes, I am ravenous.'

'Come this way . . . ' Without calling for Kendel, I marched him straight down the servants' corridor. He winked at me and we made straight for the kitchens.

Pausing by two framed photographs on the wall, I whispered to him, 'What do you make of Mrs Denton and the medication, then?'

'She is an extremely beautiful woman. She appears to be in very good health. She was disorientated, but I believe the draught she has been given is an old recipe, which includes the opiate laudanum. She may well be addicted, in a very mild way, but I did not find or see anything that would suggest it is taken in excess. However . . . ' He paused and discreetly glanced around us.

'What?' I asked.

'She was awake and, although she appeared weary, I did not see signs of a severe problem. Her eyes looked normal, and that is something you cannot pretend. There were no visible signs of bruising on her neck or lower arms or hands,' he added.

'Ivan, I am certain she does not wish to hide anything. It is the concerns of others that made me ask you to check.' He raised a solitary eyebrow at me. 'So she is not heavily drugged, then?' I could see that he seemed amused by my admission and defence of her.

He smiled at me. 'Hector, no, she is not. I thought you were worldly-wise. Don't look at her through blinkered eyes, eh? She may be beautiful, in a way that a lady should be — elegant, perhaps, would be more fitting a word — but I would not doubt the ability and agility of her quick wit. She tolerated my intrusion as Mrs Bellington was so concerned for her, but she watched me closely despite her slightly fuggy brain. Now, come on; let us be about our task, for I must get on.' He walked forward toward the warmth and bustle of the kitchen.

I was taken aback by his comment, but justified the lady's actions as natural because a strange man, doctor or not, had entered her bedchamber. She was bound to be taken aback, medication or no. Without hesitation I followed him along the corridor to the kitchen. It was sparse, whitewashed, with only two photographs of the staff on the wall. One was taken with Mr Denton Senior standing proudly in the centre of his full complement of staff. In his time there were butler, valet, footmen, housekeeper, lady's maid, cook, upper and lower maids, and more — certainly more than should any man need to look after their home. The second photo showed the current Mr Denton, deceased, standing with his butler at one side of him and the housekeeper on the other, next to Cook and a few maidservants. How times had changed. Looking at the two pictures, something seemed odd, but I couldn't think what it was.

I approached the archway and could see that cold food had been prepared for the staff. It was now well past midday, and all was being done in a sombre and quiet atmosphere. Ivy was looking like a sulky child. Ivan's focus settled upon the lad from the stable, who was curled up in a ball near the fire, anxiously scratching his arm. Mrs Elmwood was busy slicing a new loaf. She looked up at us, apparently somewhat perplexed to see us standing there. The young maid looked a little guilty as we entered; as I suspected, she had repeated my overheard comments to Cook.

'Mr Kendel is not here!' she snapped. 'I'll fetch him.' She put the knife and the bread down and wiped her hands on the cloth by her side.

'Where has he gone?' I asked, realising that he had not been pestering me or murmuring offensive comments in my direction for the best part of an hour. I had not missed them, but it made me wonder what he was up to.

'He's burning Atticus!' the lad snapped at Ivan.

'Why?' I asked.

Cook interjected. 'He didn't want the lad seeing the mess the cat was in, so he's got Baker, the groundsman, to give it a quick cremation. He could hardly let Sam bury it in flattened pieces, could he?' She glanced at Ivan, whose cheeks had flushed slightly, and then she slammed the dough mixture from her bowl onto the old wooden table. It looked aged, as if it had been there for centuries. 'What do you want now?' she asked, recovering some of her normal calmer manner back. Ivy just stood in the background, her shoulders slightly more rounded and her chin lower than it had been earlier.

'We would like a tray to be brought to the library, please; and when Mr Kendel has finished, perhaps you could send him along too.' I smiled, trying to cut through the tension.

'Ha!' She shook her head. 'Oh, he'd love that, me sending him along with the tray on your orders.' She shrugged her shoulders and nodded to me. 'You gents don't belong in here, so you best go and await your food.' She glanced up at Ivan, but her face changed from genial to serious in its expression.

He was not following her advice, but had moved further inside the large stone room. A rack with hung copper pans of various sizes was rigged above the old oak table. Behind her were the fire and the range. There was still a black iron door in the stone wall for the bread oven. The oversized flat paddle at the side told me it was still very much in use. The kitchen was a combination of newer gadgets and the very old. I guessed the thinking was that, if it wasn't broke then it hadn't needed new investment to fix it.

Ivan looked at the boy. 'I am sorry, Sam, it was an accident. I did not kill your cat intentionally, lad.'

The boy stared at him, seemingly unmoved by Ivan's gesture at peace. I guessed his cat had meant a lot to him. Poor Atticus, to have been loved so.

Ivan was watching as the lad stifled his sobs and rubbed his arm. Then he scratched at it through his sleeve. 'Are you well?' he asked.

Cook stood in front of Ivan. 'No, he

isn't. He is proper upset about that blasted cat, and I'll give him a good soak in the tub once you is gone, as he's had a right shock. So please be on your way and I'll fetch you your tray through. Best leave him to get over it in his own time. I'll find him something to do. The devil delights in sad, idle hands.'

Ivan ignored her; his attention was taken elsewhere as he was now looking around. He stepped behind Cook and opened the scullery door.

Mrs Elmwood became very agitated. 'I said I'd bring you your food. If you wants something specific, then ask, don't snoop in me larder!' Her fists were balled and resting on her hips. She was apparently not a woman who was used to being ignored or having her larder 'snooped' in. I stifled a grin.

Ivan, calm as always, continued to completely ignore her. He disappeared inside and opened his bag.

'Mrs Elmwood . . . ' he began.

'Yes, what . . . 'ere, what're you taking?' She was trying to look over his shoulder as he rummaged around, but he was tall and she short; he seemed to be tasting some small samples of sugar, flour, spice, or anything he was curious about.

When he turned around and stepped back out, he nearly knocked into her. Still ignoring her protestations, he asked her, 'Can you show me the leftovers from Mr Denton's dinner last night?'

'That I can't, because his broth has been all washed up. 'Ere, you ain't blaming my cooking, I hope. I've been cooking meals in this house for three years, and no one has been made sick by my food ever. Never has anyone dropped dead of it either! He was as drunk as they come, that's what was wrong with him, and I don't need no fancy bag of gimmicks to tell me that!' She was being very defensive to the point of open aggression.

Kendel re-emerged from the stable yard. He looked at Ivan and then glared at me. He also nodded at Mrs Elmwood, who had folded her arms and looked as annoyed as she could do without speaking to Kendel directly about her objections to us being in her space.

'Gentlemen, I am most surprised that you would blunder in here. This is not your place. Please be about your business, and leave us in peace to grieve and support Mrs Denton, for I still have to inform the mistress that her husband is dead.' He wiped his feet on a rough rug before entering.

'Surely Mrs Bellington would be doing that,' I said. 'It would be more delicate for her maid and confidante to break such grievous news, would it not?'

'I am the butler here, man, and I will be present for that horrendous moment. I would hardly expect the housekeeper to have to carry the burden herself.' He shrugged. 'Maid, indeed! I hope when you take down your interview notes you pay more attention to the detail.'

I half-grinned. I had merely wished to rile the man, but realised it did not give a professional impression of my ability, so my moment of weakness had backfired on me.

'Mrs Denton may well need her medication. She is a very sensitive lady.'

Kendel tried to usher us out, but we both stood firm.

'The cat . . . ' I began.

'Baker has burnt the poor thing's remains. Sam has the rest of the day to mourn it, and then tomorrow he will be back to his work. Better for him that way, and unlike some, he has to do an honest day's work for his keep.' He looked at the boy, but his words were softer than the ones he directed at us.

'Ivy, the scoop of broth you gave it earlier, was that the same as Mr Denton's supper?' I asked.

'Ivy, haven't I told you about feeding that bloody cat! It was always eating anything it could get its paws or claws on unless it meant actually catching it first. Bloody useless furball! No wonder it is . . . *was* too lazy to catch any mice!' Mrs Elmwood interrupted, but Ivy was now looking very anxious and nodded her answer to me. Ivan slipped away whilst I stayed and watched this small group of people — Kendel angry and defiant, Elmwood defensive and flustered, Ivy anxious and unsure.

'Have a tray brought to the library; and Kendel, I will see you in the study in half an hour. Ivy, run upstairs and tell Mrs Bellington that I would like to see Mrs Denton at three p.m.'

I about-turned and left them with Kendel cursing behind me.

Some moments later, Ivan joined me in the library. I had watched him go outside. He had retraced his steps along the drive where the accident had happened. What he picked up I do not know, but he came back in to join me with his sleeves rolled up as if he had been washing his hands. Wise after dealing with dead folk, I thought. His work was something I admired, but could never have taken to myself. My Gran had been very superstitious, especially of the dead, and even believed they walked free on Hallow's Eve, so some thread of this must have rubbed off on me. Ivan, on the other hand, was a practical man. He believed in what he could see and touch. If it could not be analysed, then he thought it a figment of the imagination.

'You think he could have been poisoned?'

I asked directly, in a lowered voice.

'I am unsure,' he said. 'It is possible.' But he shrugged as he took a seat at the table next to me. 'It is certainly a possibility, but I would need to do more tests.'

We were surrounded by books on all walls. The room was light, because of the tall Georgian windows. The heavy drapes would keep the sun from fading the older volumes, no doubt untouched by human hand for decades, if not centuries, but there they were displayed as a visible testament to the learned owners of the Hall.

'It is a strange situation here . . . ' he began. He scratched the back of his head. 'Your Mrs Denton . . . '

'She is not 'my' Mrs Denton at all,' I rebuked, but in so doing I had risen to his taunt and he smiled back at me. 'Very funny; so your point is?'

'It is just that she certainly has enough opiate to be a heavy user, but she does not show the signs of it, and yet has displayed such symptoms to her staff.' He shrugged. 'It is as though she plays some game with them, but I cannot for the life of me fathom why. Unless she suffers from some derangement of the mind . . . but she seems very sensible and lucid.' He fell quiet whilst the younger girl brought in the tray. Kendel had opened the door for her.

'Annie, isn't it?' I said, and smiled at her.

'Yes, sir,' she replied as she carefully placed the tray on the table without spilling a drop.

'You did that with great skill, Annie,' Ivan complimented her. Instantly she smiled and her eyes lit up. I do not think many people had taken the bother to flatter her in her young life.

'Thank you, sir; Mr Kendel said he thought I'd measure up well, sir, when he chose me.'

'Annie! Come on. It is not the place of a servant to chatter with the members of the household, or their 'guests',' Kendel remonstrated, and Annie's head drooped as did her shoulders as she left. Kendel shut the door firmly behind him.

'Still a bully of young girls, it appears,' Ivan commented.

The words grated on me. 'He must have shared that trait with his master. Look what I found in his drawer.' I pulled out the brown envelope and showed the doctor the photographs.

'Photography is a marvellous thing. It can capture beauty, provide evidence, and be used to catch villains; or it can be turned like anything else to disreputable dross,' he commented before turning each photograph over carefully. He was holding them by the edge. 'Still, they may be a little saucy, but I have seen much worse than these; ones that are truly vulgar. These kind of images are ten a penny in the city.'

'I obviously mix in the wrong circles,' I said dryly.

He laughed. 'Well, Hector, I do not seek them out; but where sin is concerned, crime goes hand in hand with it. When you have seen as many bodies as I, vanity is stripped away before the skin and bone. I am hardly going to be shocked that a man likes sneaking peeks at scantily-clad young women.' He shook his head at my stiff expression. I was definitely shocked by them, as I had rarely seen such images. They somehow defiled women and depraved men instead of showing their beauty. Perhaps my upbringing had been too stiff.

'True.' I put them back in the envelope and placed them in my pocket. 'I prefer having a wife to hold than an image to behold.' My response was defensive but honest.

'You are a frustrated poet, Hector.' He laughed.

'Did you find anything in the cupboards?' I asked, wanting to return my attention to the investigation in hand.

'The normal things.' He shrugged. 'Rat poison is commonly stored in such places; if I had my way, all food and toxins would be stored completely separately; but then, if you look at the basic cleaning products used daily, they too can be lethal, so where would one draw the line? There was nothing obvious, but I have samples and I have to complete tests. Therefore, to that end I shall leave you to your questioning and go and prepare. Within the hour the body will be removed.'

'Thank you, Ivan. I will stay here, so do make a telephone call if you have any lead I need to pursue.'

He grinned at me. 'Enjoy your moment, Hector. It beats chasing a thief down the docks, doesn't it?' He was too observant and knew me too well.

I winked. We had grown up in the same neighbourhood, and had too many childhood secrets to keep about each other to be anything other than close friends.

The food was good, but I ate in haste. I wanted to be sitting in the study when Kendel arrived for his interview. This would be one interrogation I would relish doing, if only to watch the insufferable man squirm as he answered questions that I would pose — and pose them I would. Then I would see Mrs Denton . . .

As I moved, the light from the window caught the edge of my simple wedding ring and it glinted. A peculiar feeling swept through me. It was as if I had been reminded as to where my loyalty and duty lay. Was I really so fickle as to waver from my Elsie, in mind if not in body? This was a distraction I did not need. I had arrived in this place a happily married man, and all manner of notions had crossed my mind as I thought of Mrs Amelia Grace Denton — a name I had placed into a dark corner of my subconscious. Or was it the effect of seeing pretty young girls, scantily-clad, in photographs, and being guilty of picturing . . . her clad likewise? I really needed to rethink my priorities.

I briskly left the room and headed hastily from the library, crossing to the study. Something was telling every fibre of my being that all was not right here, and for some reason that was crossing over into my marriage and making me question my own long-held and recently-achieved 'dream'. Yes, cobalt blue eyes had somehow penetrated my skin. A skin I was beginning to think was thinner than I had realised.

9

I took my place behind the desk. He was a few minutes late. I was expecting it, as he had to find some way to assert his own authority and position. Then the doorbell rang, and all was a hive of activity as the body was removed and taken away. I told Kendel to meet me in ten minutes once they had driven off.

When he walked in, he closed the door and sat down without a word. His eyes looked tired, drawn; he placed his hands on each of his legs, and in a resigned voice said, 'Get on with this so we can be rid of each other.' He looked genuinely sad.

'Mr Kendel, how long have you worked here?' I asked as a gentle starter.

'Twenty years. I worked my way up from nothing to a respected and responsible position. I am extremely well-thought-of by my betters.' He looked at me with no hint of arrogance for a change.

'You worked for his father first,' I continued.

'Yes!' he snapped out. There he was — the Kendel I knew. The calm one, the one that looked kindly at sad little boys, was a man I did not recognise, and yet it had been him. Perhaps I brought the past back to him. Perhaps he had moved on.

He was rapidly becoming impatient as I covered ground I already knew the answers to.

'So, how much did Mr Denton drink last night, and why?' My tone changed and I wanted to snap him. Make him blurt out something in haste.

'I am not sure on either account.' He stared directly at me, and I instinctively knew he was lying. Was he covering for his master, or covering something else?

So I tried a different line of questioning. 'How long have you known Mrs Bellington?' I softened my tone again.

'Since the day she arrived,' he replied, in a slightly lower voice himself. Was he playing with me, mimicking my tactics? Or was it because he softened whenever Mrs Bellington was there in body or name?

'She was not the housekeeper when she arrived?' I watched him closely. I decided that he was trying to play the same controlled game that I was.

'No, she was Mrs Denton's personal maid.' He sat back in the chair and began to look around the place as if distracted. I noticed how his hands and manner also relaxed when he talked of her.

'Do you have a personal understanding with Miss Ethel Bellington?' I asked innocently. He seemed torn between boasting that he did indeed have a love in his life, or dismissing it as an inappropriate question. He remained silent for a moment, just staring at me, as if deciding which way to go with this.

'Well?' I persisted.

'I have asked her to be my wife.' He shifted his weight uneasily, but there was a strange sincerity to his words.

I was impressed. I had not expected him to come straight out with that, because if she was going to refuse him, then it would be a cause of further embarrassment. I could not see this man ever taking rejection with good grace. He had quite a fall to come, but I would not gloat on that, for if my Elsie had turned me down I would have felt bereft. But she hadn't, for she had excellent taste!

'Has she accepted your offer?' I asked, knowing full well she had not.

'Not as yet. Events have overtaken us, but I am sure she will.' He raised his head. 'Unlike some people, she sees the good in me!'

'How, or should I ask, why?' I pushed, watching his face flush. He was actually embarrassed.

'Why wouldn't she? I am a man of position. I have savings and I can provide for her. A house like this still needs a butler to run it even if it has a mistress at its head. I suspect that his uncle will take it on anyway.' His chin had risen. He was trying to look down at me, but I was in every way the bigger man and we both knew it.

'His uncle?' I repeated, moving the conversation on again.

'Mr Jonathon Archibald Denton of Bristol. He has had shared business dealings with his nephew for years. He took him in and educated him as a youngster. The two have always been close. I am sure he will want to visit once things are sorted.'

'What business is he in?' I queried.

'Shipping! The family have been in the import and export business for generations,' he said proudly.

I just looked at him. I made no comment, but the thought in my head was that they would have made their money on the back of slavery. It was a history that I would never be proud of, but I was not Denton or Kendel.

'So what can you tell me about Millicent?' I changed tack.

His head shot up at this question and he sat back in the chair. 'What about the girl?'

'What is there to tell?' I persisted. 'She left.'

'Then you know about her.' He crossed his arms.

'Why? Why would a young girl who had not been here long leave?'

'She ran off with a lad from the town. Loose morals. It's the age-old tale.' He sniffed, but he was watching me closely.

'What of the other girls who also left?' I persisted.

'Have you lost leave of your senses? You are here because a man, a good man, has died, and you are asking about the goings-on of young females who should know better how to behave.' He shook his head. 'Your superiors will learn of this charade. You have turned Mr Denton's death into a double travesty.' He shook his head.

'Were they all loose in morals?' I asked.

'Not all, no; so when you have finished playing your games, then I would suggest that I return to my duties. I have yet to inform Mrs Denton, who is now awake, that she is a widow. Ethel is waiting for me.' He leaned forward as if he wished to leave. He wanted to take control of the situation again.

'That won't be necessary. I will inform her shortly,' I said, and his look should have cut me to the core, but it did not even penetrate my uniform.

'You are a heartless ba — '

I cut in. 'Coming from you, Kendel, I

find that hard to take. How many younger lads did you mercilessly torment and make their lives hell? How many have you bruised and broken to prove your superior strength and idiotic pride?' I deliberately showed my temper and disgust at him.

It worked, but not as I had expected it to. He rose to my taunt, and with his hands on the desk in front of me he leaned forward. 'They had homes to go to, mothers to hold and comfort their little sobbing faces. I had no one and nobody cared!' He sat back.

'You had a mother of your own, man; do not lie to me, Kendel.' I remembered her plainly. She was quite a sombre woman. A force of nature but she was there.

'Aye, in name I had one, but the back of her hand was harder than any man's I ever met. She knocked me about senseless. One time I lost a whole day before I came to. Aye, that one scared her, and for a whole month she let me be. But then she began again. Who could I turn to, eh? That shell of a man who was my father died when I was but seven, and she hated me for being dependent upon her. Aye, I had a mother and I wished to hell she had burnt there years before she did, so don't preach to me if I took some of my anger out on them young milksops who were doted on by their loving, caring mamas. You see, you can tell Ethel what you like about my past, because she knows it and she understands. She loves me for who I am now, and not for the person I once may have been. I'll make a good husband for her and take her away from all this serving and bowing.' He stopped and breathed deeply realising his guard had dropped completely. 'You bastard! Got what you wanted, have you? Well I don't care. You know the truth of it, so condemn me for being a heavy-handed abused lad if you must, but I had nothing to do with Mr Denton's death. He drank himself into a stupor, and that's the end of it.' He flopped back into the seat as if his energy was spent.

'Tell me who his connections are in London,' I asked.

'No! I will not.'

'You wish to obstruct a policeman in his course of duty?' I asked, and glared at him.

'No, because I can't. I do not . . . did not travel with him to London. He has a club there, and I understand that a valet is provided for the members if needed.' He sniffed. Had he felt snubbed?

'What does he do there?' I continued, seeing his unease and still reeling from his revelation regarding his childhood.

'Drink? Talk to his business contacts? I do not go with him, so how would I know?' He shrugged. 'It is a world to which the likes of us do not belong.'

So he had felt snubbed. 'You are his manservant. You would surely have some idea: betting slips, promissory notes, debts, pictures . . . '

His eyes narrowed as I listed these things.

'He gambled a little,' he replied thoughtfully.

'A lot more, perhaps, than he should?' I added.

'Who is to say how much he should?' he replied dryly. 'It is not my place . . . '

'His bank manager, his wife perhaps?'

'It is none of her business. A man has interests that do not concern women. She is provided for . . . '

'The money came from her family, did it not?' I persisted, realising that that heart of his which I had only just discovered existed was about to be shattered.

'The money is his once he marries her,' he explained. 'It is the law, surely you know that.'

'How wealthy is Ethel?' I slipped in, and watched the man opposite nearly explode in my face in denial that he was a gold-digger. I ignored his exasperation and continued. 'How — '

'Go to hell!' he shouted at me.

I didn't; I had further questions to ask. 'What property does he lease in Harrogate, and why?' I asked.

'He doesn't,' he said, as he sat back down.

'Are you certain?' I raised an eyebrow; curiously we now had a lead.

'Yes, I would know.' He seemed emphatic, and at that moment I was certain he knew nothing of the lease. Therefore, his master had withheld secrets from his devoted — and apparently blinkered — butler. But then again, why shouldn't he? He was a paid employee.

'Have you seen this before?' I placed the key with the fob showing the number 21 on the desk.

He looked at it but showed no sign of recognition. 'I have never seen it before. Where did you find it?'

'With this.' I dropped the brown paper envelope on the table. He did not seem to look shocked.

'What is in it?' he asked.

'Have you really no idea?' I persisted, but the angry look previously on his face was now one of confusion.

'No.' He reached for it, but I swept it up and kept the pictures in my pocket along with the key. I would follow up any leads on them once I had seen Mrs Denton.

'Before you go, Kendel, tell me why you burnt Atticus?'

'I didn't, but I had Baker do it, because

the remains were not a pretty sight and Sam, the lad, is a sensitive type. He was in such a state that I wanted it out of the way. If it had been in one piece, then I would have let the lad bury it, and had Baker take him off to do it.' He shrugged.

'No other reason?' I asked.

'No!' he snapped.

'Then it appears there is hope for you, and that you do have a heart after all,' I said quietly.

Kendel rose. I thought he would curse my comment as sarcasm, but to my surprise he seemed to take it literally, and I actually wondered if this man could have changed so much. Was it I who was being unjust in my condemnation of him? If his mother had really been such an ogre, then perhaps it was he who had needed help more than his victims. This was a new and surprising way of viewing the actions of the perpetrator of such violence. The line between victim and villain was suddenly blurred.

He surprised me even further when he held his hand out for me to shake across the desk. I did so automatically.

'I will not apologise for how I was, but neither am I proud of it.' He turned to leave without meeting my stunned expression.

'Please see if Mrs Bellington has Mrs Denton ready for me to see now. It is a quarter to three, and I would like to see her at three p.m. promptly.' My day was fast disappearing and I still had much to do.

'Very well.' He did not stand as straight and as tall as he had been. 'But I ask you, Blagdon, to be gentle with her.'

'Kendel, I am sorry that I was unaware that you were beaten as a child yourself.' I did not know what possessed me to offer this apology to him, but he shook his head.

'What good would it have done for you to have known? At least when people hated and feared me, they cared, I was something; but if all I had was looks of forlorn pity, how would I have coped with her until they took her away?' He peered at me and I realised there was more to tell. This man who I had despised for years had been carrying a huge emotional burden from child- to manhood. For a moment, it was I who felt small.

'They what?' I asked.

'When I was twelve, she nearly cracked the rent man's skull open with a fire iron, and was taken away to the madhouse as insane. She died there five years later. You see, I was free of her then.' He shrugged, but I doubted if the weight of such an ordeal could be disposed with so easily.

I was quite speechless. I had been too lost in my own tragedies, within my own dismal past, to have looked around and seen those that others were coping with. He had now set his sights on another woman. Ethel Bellington. He had no idea she was one of those firebrand types also who wanted the vote and the place of a man. I was certain she had no intention of settling for him. How near to the surface was that temper of his? How soon would he erupt when he found out that the 'love' he thought was for him was actually understanding and concern felt for the young child that he had been? Perhaps she felt sorry for him, but no more wanted him than his headstrong and violent mother. Kendel was in for more pain, for I could not see a happy ending in this relationship.

He left the room. I stood and combed my hair, looking in the mirror. It was a dark mass of chocolate brown, that was what my Elsie said. She liked the fact that it was not straight and waved slightly, but I didn't. It had a tendency to flick in opposite ways to what I wanted it to go, but she loved playing with it when it was freshly-washed and springy. I smiled; she was full of such playful notions.

10

Approaching the morning room, I could hear two women's voices, and knew them to be Mrs Denton and Mrs Bellington. My eyes were mesmerised by the sight of Mrs Denton standing by the window in a delicate navy silk afternoon dress. A number of covered buttons decorated the front, contouring her bust line in two fine rows, with matching coloured lace around the sleeves, front and neck. I knew little of women's finery and fashion, but I could admire the poise and effect a well-dressed woman had on a man when she carried it off with such confidence. The green sash belt matched the colour of her eyes, and the whole outfit flattered her honey-blonde hair, which had been carefully dressed. The plainer skirt lengthened the woman's fine figure as it hung almost to the floor.

Remembering myself and my rank, not to mention my purpose, I strode into the room as confidently as I could.

Mrs Bellington's navy dress was, by contrast, much starker. The two could not project such a different presence of rank and character, but both were strong, modern women in a modern world. I thought the likes of Kendel should definitely feel threatened, but I welcomed it. I did not see why men should carry the burden of all things; women were very capable. My mother had been a model of organisation and survival to emulate once Father and Jeb had so cruelly been taken from us.

'Ah, Mr Blagdon, what a pleasure it is to see you again. Tell me, Chief Inspector, how is that delightful little wife of yours?' She gracefully gestured to the chair by the fire so that I should sit down.

'You flatter me, Mrs Denton; I am but a Sergeant,' I said calmly.

'Perhaps you are now, but someone of your intelligence and of such fine build, I am sure will be an Inspector soon enough,' she said as she too sat down opposite me.

'My wife is very well,' I answered and

sat back down. I was not a green recruit, and the words of flattery should not have ruffled me in any way, but she played a devilishly wicked game. Part of me felt as though I should insist upon standing; part of me wanted to sit on the two-seater settee with her; and part of me rankled that she had referred to my Elsie as my 'little wife'. It was somehow belittling — literally — and after all my desire to meet with Mrs Amelia Grace Denton again, it seemed strange that in her opening greeting she had somehow insulted my wife, and that felt so wrong.

I was also surprised because here was a woman who, although looking paler and more tired than she had been last year, did not seem drugged at all. Her words seemed most astute.

'Sergeant Blagdon, I will be honest with you as you are an officer of the law, and a man that I respect.' She looked at me and smiled quickly, then returned to her sombre pose. 'I have been informed that poor Bartholomew passed away last night.' She swallowed and was gracious enough to look down.

So apparently neither I nor Kendel would have the opportunity to tell her. I was disappointed, as I had wanted to witness her initial response and watch those eyes of hers. I was speechless. How could she keep such a controlled air about her at such a time?

'I knew that he had a 'problem', and I hope that you will do your best to make sure that the truth does not become the local gossip.' She sniffed, and Mrs Bellington placed a comforting hand upon her mistress's shoulder as she stood behind her chair.

'Yes, he has a 'problem' in that he is dead, Mrs Denton,' I said. If it sounded sarcastic, it was not meant to be. It was meant as an astonishing fact that I was unsure she fully understood or comprehended.

'Yes!' she snapped. Mrs Bellington patted the woman's shoulder and then Mrs Amelia Grace Denton breathed in deeply. Her corseted figure, already upright, seemed to take on an even stiffer countenance. But then something striking happened as she revealed a more caring, grieving face to me. It would have convinced me if her previous manner had not been so genuine.

'I was referring to his drinking,' she explained. 'He could be quite . . . awkward when he had over-imbibed.' She swallowed gracefully and then dabbed the corner of her eye with her gloved finger. Ever so gracefully . . . 1 wondered if she ever lost her poise. Like an eggshell, it could be tough and protective, or shatter if pressure was applied to its vulnerable sides. I wondered if she ever swore and ranted, wailed and cried, or laughed a heartily joyous laugh that made a man's heart stop still in the moment he shared her joy. My Elsie did. She was just as she was: no games, no pretences, and certainly no false tears. I knew then how much I loved my Elsie, and my obsession with this woman dispersed with that one false gesture. I realised that she had only really viewed me as a puppet, a new toy with which she could play. Oh, how much Blagdon still had to learn about people!

'Your grief must be deep, but you handle it well, Mrs Denton. Could you enlighten me as to when you last spoke to your husband?' I watched as she straightened the fabric of her skirt with the palm of her right hand — it followed the contour of her thigh. Was she flirting with me or trying to distract me? Surely I had not shown how I felt about her at the fair? What a fool I must have looked; but then I had been happy, relaxed, and flattered that she would choose to walk by the river with me. I thought her lonely, and she must have seen me as a simple distraction when she had been bored. Since then, I had realised that a policeman should not let their guard down even when off-duty.

'Well . . . ' She paused pensively. ' . . . it would be before he went to his study after dinner. I had been tired after the drive from Harrogate, and so I retired early and had my medication.' She looked down at the delicate hands nestled in her lap as if it was a shameful admission. *Insincerity* was the word that crossed my mind.

'What had you been doing in Harrogate?' I asked.

'I had been shopping. Bartholomew had some business there.' She yawned, and then looked at me apologetically and smiled. 'I found the most exquisite brooch — an opal in the centre of a golden flower!'

'What business would that be?' I persisted, ignoring her enthusiasm for her trinket. Opals were bad luck; my Elsie would say they were God's tears. I had always dismissed such superstitious rot, but looking at this woman, I thought they had not brought her good fortune in life.

'His business? Whatever would I be interested in that for? No, I had an appointment at the milliners too. They can be devilishly tiring, as fittings can take hours to complete when one is planning for a tour.' She smiled with even more enthusiasm as she talked of her plans. They were like water off a duck's back to me, as I could no more visualise her life than she could living mine.

'A tour?' I repeated.

'Yes, we were planning on visiting the United States of America; but of course, after the tragedy of the *Titanic*, we changed our minds and decided we would venture to Spain and Italy. Imagine

Rome in the summer!' She looked at me with eyes that sought understanding.

I tried, but Scarborough was the best I could do these days.

'Of course, that will all change now. Once the funeral is over, I shall consider taking a year out in Boston, I think. I have family there, and I promised Bellington I'd take her one day.' She sniffed. 'It is so sad. He was once so kind before the desire for liquor took hold of his soul. Will it be long before we can arrange things?' She stared at me through moist eyes. 'I have many things to sort out. I need to be with my family as soon as possible. I need them to help me through my grieving.'

My stomach was turning — not in knots of desire, rather in fits of disgust. 'I could not say. It all depends what the post-mortem shows up,' I explained. She cared nothing for the estate. Its workers needed it to survive. She had people depending upon her for their livelihoods, yet she thought only of her own comfort.

'I have not given consent for any such examination,' she said, and for the first time showed what I considered to be the first sign of genuine concern.

'It is not yours to give, Mrs Denton. You see, we are unclear as to what actually caused his death, or what happened to him beforehand, and therefore we need to examine him further,' I explained, and got the distinct impression that at last her opinion of me was changing, and she no longer viewed me in the same light.

'Whatever can you mean?' She stood up; so did I.

'I mean just what I say, Mrs Denton. We are uncertain of the facts and the circumstances of your husband's death, and therefore nothing will be arranged for his funeral until such time as we have the results of the post-mortem. We all want to know the truth, do we not?' I asked, and I saw a very dark cloud cross her face.

She looked at Mrs Bellington. 'What does this mean?' she repeated. 'Do I not have the authority over what happens regarding my own husband's funeral?'

'It means there will be no trips or tours until we have some answers as to why your husband died in his bed, Mrs

Denton.' My reply was greeted by an icy glare that would have cut through most men, but I had recovered my wits and stood still whilst Mrs Denton stormed out of the room.

Mrs Bellington did not immediately go after her. Instead, she stood holding the back of the chair, as if deep in thought.

'For a lady who is supposed to be weakened by delicate nerves and under medication, she seems to have a very clear mind,' I commented.

'Forgive me for saying so, but she does not cope with reality very well. She was brought up in a very cosseted way, in a wealthy Boston family, and is used to being provided for and having people to see that her needs are met. This has come as a complete shock to her. The marriage has been a relatively short one, and her plans for a more enlightened time in Europe, hopefully taking her husband away from his clubs and alcohol, have been shot down in flames.' She was being straightforward and honest again. I had more admiration for her character than for her mistress's.

'I think Mr Denton's plans were shot further down, don't you?' I responded, finding it difficult to find any sympathy for the tantrums of an overgrown spoilt brat.

She shook her head, but was smiling. 'I did not think that you would understand her; you are far too practical a man for her fanciful notions.'

I was hardly going to be impressed by the assertions of Mrs Bellington. I certainly could be fanciful, if the opportunity presented itself. However, I needed to work and be 'practical'. I can only presume my fanciful mind must have been working overtime when I met Mrs Denton the previous summer. Or perhaps it had been the combined effect of Elsie's homemade punch and the lovely summer's day.

'So, when will you shoot Mr Kendel's dreams down in flames?' I asked quietly as she passed me to follow Mrs Denton.

'That is a personal question, and one that is between me and Mr Kendel. I may seek for women to have the vote, but I do not dislike gentlemen, Mr Blagdon; and for all his past failings, Mr Kendel is a true 'gentle man' at heart.'

I stayed quiet, for I did not wish to express my own feelings regarding the man. Even though I now knew his reasons for his behaviour, it still showed a dark side to his character that I was unsure he had completely outgrown.

I heard the telephone's bell ringing and made my way to the study. Kendel was there already.

'Leaham Hall,' he announced in a very artificial tone. 'Yes, I shall get him. Who shall I say is calling? Very well, sir, I shall fetch him forthwith.' His voice was louder than normal as he shouted his words into the mouthpiece. Then he stepped away and gestured to me to come forward.

'It is for you; a Police Constable Higgins.' He gripped a pencil from the desk and stood back.

'Sorry, Kendel, I must ask you to leave the room,' I said as I picked up the receiver and straightened the cord, waiting for him to close the door.

'Yes, Sergeant Blagdon here,' I said, and hoped that PC Jack Higgins had found out something interesting for me.

'I looked up that address you gave me, and the housing agents told me it is for the rental of a room at 21 Fairview Street, sir. I telephoned the Harrogate branch and spoke to a colleague who owed me a good turn. He said it was quite near and went around to the place. It appears to be rented out to a photographer. That is what the neighbour said.' The line crackled.

'Was anyone there?' I asked.

'No, sir, but the neighbour said that the lady often calls on a Thursday.'

The line crackled and whirred, but I was not sure I had heard correctly. 'The lady?' I repeated.

'Yes, sir.'

'Any mention of a man?' It did not seem right to me that a lady would take such photographs. Besides, it was usually a man's business. I cringed inwardly, as Elsie would no doubt have corrected me and told me that women could do just the same as men, use their hands and brains, except men were needed for heavy labour. Women these days had ideas and notions about such things.

'Yes, sir, he is normally there on Mondays and Tuesdays and the occasional Thursday.'

'Did you get the names?' I wanted the answer to be as it came.

'The gentleman is a Mr B.L. Denton; and the lady, unfortunately not yet, but she comes with one of her maids.'

'Keep digging and, if you can, get authorisation to search it. Mr Denton is dead. Find out what he has in there. I will be back at the station tomorrow.'

'Yes, sir.'

I replaced the receiver and wondered how many women Denton had had in his life.

I sat back, pulled out the photographs from the envelope, and looked at them again one by one. Ivan was quite correct: these were no more than slightly saucy pictures of pretty girls, even tasteful compared to some. He did me an injustice as to my experience. I too had heard of much worse through my days in the force, abuse of a lovely invention.

Did Denton just dabble in photography

as some sort of fantasy? And if these were taken in Harrogate, why did one have a photographer's name from London on the back?

The hall clock struck four. The day was slipping away. I wanted to ask so much more, but would have to leave it and return tomorrow after I had checked in at the station. There was something I was missing, the familiarity of the photograph of the smartly-dressed girl.

'Yes!' Sometimes something just clicks in your brain, like the click on the telephone line before you are connected, and this was such a moment. I walked briskly to the servants' corridor and stood in front of the photographs on the wall. One of the faces was the same as the smartly-dressed girl.

'Haven't you got a home to go to?' Mrs Elmwood's voice broke across my thoughts.

'Tell me who these girls are?' I asked innocently.

She came over to my side and stared at the group. 'Well, that one there is Sarah, that one Millicent, and you know Ivy.'

'Has Millicent ever been to London

with the Dentons?' I asked.

'No, never. The furthest she went was on a shopping trip to Harrogate with Mrs Denton. They can be quite generous when they want to be. They occasionally take one of the girls with them and let them see how the other half lives in the big town. Young Ivy went a couple of weeks ago and came back full of notions. Think it went a bit to her head. She's not settled back in here since. I suppose now she will calm herself and settle to things again. That's if Mrs Denton keeps us all on.'

'Did Mrs Bellington go with them?' I continued. I had to find out who the other woman was.

'No, sir, she was here as they had guests coming and she had to oversee that the rooms were ready. Don't think she was too pleased, being missed out again, but she was made housekeeper and so it was her duty to stay here.'

'How long was this before Millicent left the Hall?' I asked, deciding that the insistence she was made housekeeper could have been very convenient for them. Mrs Bellington was a very quick-witted lady, and so had to be kept away from this address.

'Now you're asking. Let me see, it was a weekday, because the party was arriving on the Saturday . . . Thursday, I think; and then she was here helping through their visit, which lasted about two weeks, so it must have been another two weeks after that. Yes, because Mr Denton had to go to London for a few days in between. Why, do you think you know where she is?' Her eyes lit up.

I looked down at her hopeful eyes and felt sorry that I could not reply with a simple yes.

'Not yet, but I am making enquiries, and hopefully I will be able to shed some light soon.'

She swallowed. 'Thank you, sir.'

'Now, I must be on my way. Please inform your mistress I will want to speak with her again tomorrow.'

'Yes, sir,' she said, and returned to the kitchen.

I was going to retrieve my bicycle when an idea occurred to me. I took the photograph of the Dentons and their staff down, and walked to the kitchen.

'Mrs Elmwood, have you a cloth I could wrap this in? I wish to borrow it and return it tomorrow.' Fortunately it was no more than about twelve inches by ten with a very light frame.

She happily wrapped it in a large square of muslin and tied it with string. On the cycle home, I decided that tomorrow morning I would go straight into Harrogate after reporting my findings.

11

Higgins and I arrived at 21 Fairview Street just before eleven the next day. I knocked on the neighbour's door and we waited whilst the lady opened it. She looked most disturbed to find two policemen standing before her. I presumed her to be in her fifties. She wore an old-fashioned dress of dark grey, but her eyes were bright and she seemed very astute.

'PC Higgins,' she said. 'Is there a problem? I told you all I knew yesterday.' She folded her arms in front of her.

'Indeed, and that was most helpful,' I said as I unwrapped the photograph and held it in front of me.'

She looked at it, her curiosity aroused.

'Can you tell me if you can recognise anyone on this photograph as a visitor to number twenty-one, or the gentleman, anyone at all?' I held it up for her to catch the best light in the limited hallway.

She squinted and took hold of it, studying it carefully then. Her expression changed and she nodded. 'Yes, certainly that there is the photographer.' She pointed to Mr Denton. 'That is one of the girls he brought here . . . ' She pointed to Millicent. ' . . . and that is another one . . . ' She pointed to Sarah. ' . . . and that is the girl with the striking eyes that was here a week last Thursday.'

So I knew for certain that Ivy had been here, as I had suspected.

But the woman was not done. She continued, 'And that is the lady who comes on Thursdays sometimes,' pointing to Mrs Denton.

'Thank you. Is there anyone else on the photograph that you recognise?' I asked, as Kendel's face was clear to see, but she was shaking her head. So he appeared to have nothing to do with this business, whatever lurid affair it was. But he did fetch the girls from orphanages at Denton's request. So, in my estimation, he still had something to do with it.

'Very well, thank you for your help,' I said, and recovered the photograph, exchanging a satisfied look with PC Higgins.

'You're welcome,' she said, and as we turned away she withdrew.

We proceeded to number 21.1 opened the first door off the hallway with the key from Denton's own drawer. It fit like a glove.

Inside was a small boxroom. Opposite was a sash window, to my left a sheet hung on the wall like a poorly painted canvas, and in front of this was a table and plant atop it. There was a small desk in the corner of the room, and a door to a second room. This much smaller room was dark with no window, and I realised it had been used for developing the photographs. A filing cabinet was tucked away in the corner. I switched on the light to discover an array of developing trays, lines and clips. The photographic equipment was stored neatly along one wall. It was not elaborate, but adequate to take a reasonable image.

'Try the desk out there, Jack, and see if you can come up with any connection to a Victor Braham of London.'

'Yes, sir,' he answered, and was swift about his task.

I, meanwhile, looked at the files. It seemed that Denton enjoyed taking photographs as a hobby. Nothing seemed sordid or untoward . . . until I remembered my father's advice about checking for unseen compartments.

I looked at the depth of the drawers, and realised that the bottom one was shallower on the inside than it was on the outside. It did not take me long to unlatch the false bottom and discover a long, thin, black ledger. That was when our visit to this simple office turned a dark and disturbing corner.

12

What we found merited further investigation. For one thing, there was medication — laudanum — the tincture of opium. Now I understood why Mrs Denton was not as drugged as the staff thought she should be. The medication bought for her was being used here. It was perhaps to relax the girls, or to help them once they were taken to their next location. Why else would he have it there? My stomach churned worse than it had at the most gruelling post-mortem I had witnessed. If this was true . . . if the man was not stealing his wife's medication, then surely it must mean that Mrs Denton was up to her neck in this business — the business of trading young girls!

With the letters, ledger and new photographs, we returned to the station. I was anxious to report what I had found to the Chief Constable, but wanted to talk to Ivan first. I met him outside his dissecting room, as I always referred to it.

'Any joy?' I asked. I had to block out thoughts of Mrs Denton. Amelia Grace was no more a figure of my fantasy-perfect woman. She had grown horns, a long tail, and held a pitchfork in my mind. And me — I wore the face of a fool. Taken in and duped like a lad still wet behind the ears. She might be clever, she might be beautiful . . . but my Elsie could knock her into a cocked hat when it came to true grace. My Elsie had heart and spirit and kindness, and I wanted this business done with so I could return to her and tell her so.

'Do you wish to see?' Ivan teased, knowing I preferred not to. It was the smell of his work that I had difficulty stomaching.

'Ivan, time is running by us at a fast pace.' I wanted to rush him. I wanted the answers to back the facts — or facts to back the answers — either way, I wanted a conclusive definitive result. I was to be disappointed.

We entered his small office and he closed the door. 'The man had a damaged liver from drinking too much for too long. He also had a fair amount the previous evening. To cut to the chase, Hector, there was no sign of him being held or attacked. No strangulation bruises, though he did asphyxiate, and there was no obvious blockage in his airways when I dissected them. I suspected poisoning, but of the tests available to me I can dismiss arsenic and, cyanide. What I am left with is only a possible cause of death, and my report will have to say 'inconclusive'.'

'Damnation, man. Mrs Denton was providing drugs to the husband so that the girls could become users, I suppose. Oh, this case stinks more than that bloody corpse. So what are you left with?' I asked, desperate for a direction to go to find the truth.

'You are not making sense, but you can explain later. I have found Aconitum Napellus,' he said, and I shrugged my shoulders. 'That is impossible.'

'Explain, please?' I urged.

'Monkshood, or wolfsbane. The root can be mistaken for — and unintentionally used as — Jerusalem artichoke or horseradish, and the leaf for wild garlic. If taken internally, the victim will vomit badly, go numb after tingling, have itching sensations, and then die of asphyxiation. The cat's vomit showed signs of poisoning — I checked to see if it had coughed a furball up. I duplicated a small test from a case some years ago where the affected vomit was fed to a mouse. It became ill, as there was insufficient toxin to kill it.'

'So he was poisoned!' I said excitedly.

'No, we cannot say or prove it. The cat might have eaten some rat poison, and that is as far as I can say. It had some of the same broth that Denton had the night before, but I cannot prove the link. I merely managed to save a sample from the drive as I left. None of my theories are provable — only possible.'

'But if it was poisoning that killed him, who did it?' My mind was reeling. Mrs Elmwood? The cook would be the obvious person to look at first. She prepared the food, so had the opportunity, and was unhappy and suspicious about the vanishing maids. Was this a possible motive? She had also been annoyed that the cat had been fed the broth — why?

'Speak with Mrs Elmwood about where she got her ingredients for the broth. You see, you also have to prove that this was a deliberate mistake — and not a genuine one. Barring a discovery by your investigation, or a confession, I will have to write an inconclusive report, which will mean there will be no case to answer here. Therefore, the body will be released to the family for burial.' He shrugged dismissively. 'What have you turned up?' he asked me.

'Oh, there is a charge to be answered, but the main culprit was Denton himself. He has been plucking young girls from orphanages; using the drug — his wife's medication — to subdue them, no doubt. They'd been training them for six months, to feeding them up and introducing them to the demands of domestic service. At least, that was my guess. Then he takes a pretty picture of them — not the scantily-clad ones, but so they think it is being sent off to a house of a lord in

London, to be selected for interviews as a lady's maid, or some such tale. All a big secret, I suspect.' I hated the dead man for his misuse of innocence. 'No doubt, once they are in the city, they are at the mercy of his associates from his club. I presume they are ill-used, but I have no proof, and that is what I must find to save them if at all possible.' I needed a trail to follow to see if my suspicions were true.

'So, what is he doing — was he doing, then?' Ivan asked. He had finished his portion of the investigation, and would now help if needed with the part that was mine. But on this case, I was almost done.

'I found letters written to Victor Braham, requesting certain types of young women: fair, slim, and so on, with dates for meeting at his club in London. Bidders being arranged . . . '

'The bastard!' Ivan was as outraged as I. 'Can you trace them — rescue any of them?'

'They did not stand a chance. Lambs with no connections being sent to the wolves. They were being treated like prize horseflesh. Ivy was indeed a lucky girl.' I thought about how disappointed she had been, and wondered if she would ever realise her good fortune. 'You finish your report and I will head back. We need the Yard to become involved, and the Chief Constable to authorise further investigation.' I opened the door. 'If they take us locals seriously and act swiftly, we can nab them, whatever position of rank they are in.'

'Hector,' he said. 'Well done.'

'I'm not done yet.' I left.

★ ★ ★

With the Chief Constable feeding the details of our leads to Scotland Yard, I completed my report.

'You have done amazingly well, Blagdon. I think it is time you put that old penny-farthing of yours aside and we got you a motorised one, eh?' he said, and laughed as I could not hide my joy.

'Thank you, sir,' I said, and walked out of the room a happy man. I had just achieved another life's goal. It appeared I would have to look higher in future. Wait till I told my Elsie!

13

Early the next morning, PC Harris and I returned by car back to Leaham Hall to complete my investigation. This was now much more serious than assessing a case of sudden death. The dead man had been a criminal lowlife, and I was about to nail his accomplices.

Kendel greeted us at the door as he saw us drive up. There was already another Ford T there, so I dearly hoped we were not going to clash with Mrs Denton's social circle. She had been one of the biggest surprises and disappointments in my life. She had known of his business in Harrogate — so did she understand the sordid fate of the girls or not? Did Mrs Amelia Grace Denton actually care?

'Blagdon, you could have phoned ahead,' Kendel said as he opened the car door.

I handed him the staff photograph. 'You have visitors?' I asked.

'Dr Marks,' he explained.

'Is Mrs Denton under her medication again?' I queried, hoping it was not the case, as I had questions still to ask her — important ones that could end in her arrest. The thought of that graceful woman serving time in jail saddened me, but that would not stop me from doing my job. Justice would be served.

'No, the young lad. He's fine now, but he was so upset that he's been quite ill. The doctor said he should make a full recovery.'

I nodded. Harris stepped out.

'PC Harris will need the keys to Mr Denton's desk and cabinets and drawers.'

'Why?' Kendel asked.

'We have reason to believe that Mr Denton's business affairs were not totally honourable.' I nodded to Harris and we walked in.

Kendel provided a large keyring with an assortment of keys on it. I left Harris to get to work. He had an eye for detail, and what we already had would be enough to catch the London contacts, if the Yard acted promptly. They merely had to turn up at the next venue, where Ivy was meant to have been presented, and they would catch the bidders red-handed.

'Kendel, why were you sent to collect these girls?' We had walked into the library. I showed him the picture of Millicent and watched him closely. He took it to the window as if he did not believe what he was seeing.

'It's Millicent!' he exclaimed. 'Has her Tommy found gold or something?' he asked incredulously.

Tommy, a big chap, a farmer's son, had travelled with her, but that was just to get her to London safely. He was hired by Denton, his reward being to work as a footman in a 'big house', as his mother had proudly boasted.

'So how much do you know of what happened to them?' I asked.

'I told him to pick the uglier ones, then they'd stay longer, but he just laughed at me.'

Kendel handed the photograph back to me and shook his head. He obviously had no knowledge of what had been happening; he had just obeyed the master whom he adored.

'I need to talk to Mrs Denton,' I said, but in the back of my mind a niggling doubt was rising: one I hoped was not true. The lad had been scratching at his arm. He too had licked the broth, and now had been ill. 'Please ask her to come down, and I will have a quick word with Mrs Elmwood whilst she makes herself ready.'

Kendel looked at me. 'You are not going to tell me what is happening, are you?'

'Not yet, for I believe it is in your best interests not to know.'

He gave an ironic laugh. 'Since when have you had my best interests at heart?' he asked.

'Since I became a police officer — I have everyone's best interests at heart, except for those who break the law and would hurt or entrap others.' I said no more.

14

I made my way to the servants' quarters as Dr Marks was just leaving.

'Sir, how is your patient?' I asked, genuinely hoping that he was well.

'He will make a full recovery.' He looked up at me as he pulled on his gloves.

'What was wrong with him?'

'Gastroenteritis, but he's a strong lad. Now that Mr Kendel has purchased a new kitten for him, he has perked up no end.' He smiled at me, and I had to again admit that the man was showing a compassionate side to his nature that I never would have thought possible.

'Could he have eaten something toxic?' I asked.

'Who knows? A lad may forage berries or climb trees — who knows what they might brush against? No, he will be fine. Not to worry.' He nodded to someone behind me, and I turned to see Ivy and Mrs Elmwood, both looking somewhat more anxious than when I had left them two days earlier.

'Thank you, Dr Marks,' Mrs Elmwood said and the doctor left.

I followed them back into the kitchens. They both stared at me.

'Are either of you going to ask me why I enquired about the poison?' It seemed an obvious question.

Mrs Elmwood sat in the old chair by the oven. 'Ivy, be a love; go and fetch Mrs Denton's tray down.'

The cook stared at me. She looked tired, strained, like she had been through an emotional time over the lad.

'I know what you think, and it wasn't like that.' She looked up at me.

'Tell me what it was like.'

'Young Sam, silly boy, he was supposed to stay out of them woods. He was supposed to not eat stuff growing. He thought that the wild garlic was safe, but he mixed it with something else and it made him sick. Silly boy,' she said again, and sniffed.

'Did you put it in Mr Denton's broth?' I asked.

Her head shot up.

'What you saying?' She stood up. 'You tell me where my girls are, and stop casting aspersions. There was nothing in my broth that was bad, or else me and Mrs Bellington would both be dead.'

'I have to ask,' I explained, trying not to panic her.

'Well, you've asked.' She stormed out. The truth of her girls' fates would be hard for her to fathom. I felt for the woman because she clearly cared deeply for them.

Ivy stood in the doorway, and her cobalt blue eyes were moist with unshed tears.

'Ivy . . . '

'She didn't touch the broth after she'd served the staff. I added a bit of extra flavour to it for the master. He liked his with extra garlic and pepper, he couldn't taste it without; but no one else had those. I . . . ' She sobbed.

I took the tray off her and sat her down in the chair. 'Nothing is clear about what caused his death, Ivy. The investigation is now about something else. You sit here and gather your wits. If you have done no intentional wrong, then do not worry about it. If you are questioned further, it will be in regards to the photograph you have had taken.'

I watched her eyes light up through her fear. 'It is pretty, isn't it?' she said, and wiped a tear away.

'What did Mrs Denton tell you about it?' I asked, deliberately trying to uncover how deep Mrs Amelia Grace Denton was entrenched in the business.

'That it was for Mr Denton's friend in London who wanted a lady's maid for his wife.' She sniffed. 'But that will never happen now.' The tears persisted, and the light in those beautiful eyes temporarily faded.

★ ★ ★

With a very troubled heart, I entered the morning room, where Mrs Denton was already seated. Mrs Bellington stood behind her chair.

I walked in and showed her the picture of Millicent without saying a word. Mrs Bellington looked as surprised as Kendel had.

'Sergeant Blagdon, you are full of surprises.' Mrs Denton ignored the photograph and looked at me.

'Do you know where and why this was taken, and who is in the photograph?' I asked. Mrs Bellington was staring at me as if trying to puzzle out what was happening. She, like Kendel, knew nothing of the master's business with the girls.

'Yes; my husband is a keen photographer, and he asked Millicent to pose so that she could be sent to London for an interview.' She shrugged. 'But the girl ran off with a farmer instead. So ungrateful.' She sniffed and looked away.

'Do you know what happens to the girls you took to that office?' I persisted.

'I do not care for your tone, but that is of no concern to me. I humoured my husband's hobby, which is all. He saw himself as a father figure to them, and sought out better positions within society. It was to be a life-changing opportunity for them.'

'For a fee — a hefty fee,' I added, and Mrs Bellington stepped back, her hand going to her mouth as she realised the meaning and gravity of my words.

'I do not concern myself with my husband's business affairs.' Mrs Denton stood up. 'Bellington, we are leaving.'

'You knew!' Bellington snapped at her mistress. 'You knew the truth of it.'

Yes! I was elated. I had played my hunch, and it was paying off. The Dentons' despicable treatment of their maids would not sit well with someone who wanted the vote for women.

'Bellington!' Mrs Denton snapped.

'You told Mr Kendel the precise type of girl you wanted to replace the last one who had left — you knew! That's why I always had something to do here when you took them to Harrogate!' Mrs Bellington looked shocked and enraged.

'I am telephoning my lawyer now!' Mrs Denton snapped. 'Bellington, you are sacked!'

'PC Harris,' I called. He had an armful of files and ledgers when he appeared. 'Put those in the motor car, and then escort Mrs Denton to the vehicle; she will be returning to the station with us directly.'

Kendel appeared. He saw the distress on Mrs Bellington's face and held out a hand to her. 'Ethel?'

She took it, and stood close to him. 'Oh, Mr Kendel, we have been such fools,' she said.

'Kendel, get the car. We are leaving forthwith!' Mrs Denton ordered, and made to walk briskly from the room. I blocked her.

'Try moving further, and I will manacle you myself and take you to the station in cuffs,' I told her.

She stopped, struck dumb by this sudden dose of reality.

* * *

It was late when I finished at the station. Ivan was going to return a verdict of death by natural causes due to alcohol poisoning, as he could not prove anything else. Mrs Denton was arrested for her part in the despicable scandal of providing a supply of young women to Mr Denton's associates. Scotland Yard managed to trace Millicent to a club near St

James, where she had been abused, but the search had gone cold for the others.

I felt no joy in solving this case. Bright cobalt eyes had dimmed and an innocent face had become worldlier. Even though Ivy had been spared the fate of the other young women, she had grown up and had her dreams shattered. Time would be needed to rekindle her former spirit. For Denton, it had been an easy way to make money, and his twisted mind had enjoyed playing godfather to trusting, hungry, innocent ambition. For his wife, it was a game to keep her occupied and provide the lifestyle she was used to. She cared nothing about the servants — they were replaceable.

I closed the station door behind me, thought of the look of love shared between Bellington and Kendel, and knew they had at last found each other. I pushed off on my bicycle and felt the cold air on my face, but warmth in my heart as each turn of the pedals brought me nearer to my Elsie and our lovely home — my dream achieved.

WHO IS JACQUELINE?

Victor Rousseau

After following a lone husky on the street, Paul Hewlett encounters the dog's owner — a beautiful young woman in furs, who is then savagely set upon by two strangers who attempt to abduct her. Thanks to Paul and the faithful hound, the would-be kidnappers are repelled, and he takes the mysterious woman — Jacqueline — to his apartment, leaving her there to sleep. But on returning, he discovers a grisly tableau: Jacqueline clutching a blood-stained knife, with a dead man at her feet . . .

We do hope that you have enjoyed reading this large print book.

Did you know that all of our titles are available for purchase?

We publish a wide range of high quality large print books including:

Romances, Mysteries, Classics
General Fiction
Non Fiction and Westerns

Special interest titles available in large print are:

The Little Oxford Dictionary
Music Book, Song Book
Hymn Book, Service Book

Also available from us courtesy of Oxford University Press:

Young Readers' Dictionary
(large print edition)
Young Readers' Thesaurus
(large print edition)

For further information or a free brochure, please contact us at:
Ulverscroft Large Print Books Ltd.,
The Green, Bradgate Road, Anstey,
Leicester, LE7 7FU, England.
Tel: (00 44) 0116 236 4325
Fax: (00 44) 0116 234 0205